A WORLD OF FABLES

Brenda Deen Schildgen
Georges Van Den Abbeele

Pacific View Press
Berkeley, California

Text copyright © 2003 Brenda Deen Schildgen and Georges Van Den Abbeele
Cover and interior design by Nancy Ippolito
ISBN 1-881896-27-7
All rights reserved. No part of this book may be used or reproduced, stored in a retrieval system, or transmitted, in any form or by any means, electronic, mechanical, photocopying, recording, or otherwise without prior permission in writing from the publisher. Address inquiries to Pacific View Press, P.O. Box 2697, Berkeley, CA 94702 or e-mail:pvp2@mindspring.com. Website: www.pacificviewpress.com
Printed in the United States of North America

Library of Congress Cataloging-in-Publication Data

Schildgen, Brenda Deen, 1942-
A world of fables / Brenda Deen Schildgen, Georges Van Den Abbeele.
p. cm.
ISBN 1-881896-27-7 (pbk.)
1. Fables. I. Van den Abbeele, Georges. II. Title.
PN981 .S35 2003   2003001135

The following have granted permission for reproductions and reprints: Bancroft Library, University of California, for illustrations by Oudry from *Fables de la Fontaine*, edition of Desaint and Saillant (Paris: 1755).

"The Mice that Set the Elephants Free," "Spot's Captivity," and "The Four Treasure Seekers," from *The Panchatantra*, trans. Arthur W. Ryder copyright © The University of Chicago Press.

"The Elephant Who Challenged the World" from *Fables for Our Time* copyright © 1940 by James Thurber. Copyright © renewed 1968 by Helen Thurber and Rosemary A. Thurber. "Variations on a Theme" from *Further Fables for Our Time* copyright © 1958 by James Thurber. Copyright © renewed 1984 by Helen Thurber and Rosemary A. Thurber. Reprinted by arrangement with Rosemary A. Thurber and the Barbara Hogenson Agency. All rights reserved.

Parallax Press for "The Monkey and the Crocodile" and "The Golden Deer," from the *Jataka Tales*, versions of Rafe Martin. University of Toronto Press for "Prologue," "The Wolf and the Lamb," "The Crow and the Fox," "The Lion and the Mouse," "The Crow in Peacock's Feathers," "The Beetle," "Epilogue" from Marie de France, *Fables*.

Oneworld Press for "The Unseen Elephant," from *Tales of Mystic Meaning: Selections From the Mathnawi of Jalal-ud-Din Rumi*, trans. and intro. Reynold A. Nicholson.

Pennsylvania State University Press for "The Fable of the Dog Which Was Carrying a Piece of Meat in His Mouth" and "The Fable of the Lion Which Killed Himself in Anger" from Juan Ruiz, *The Book of Good Love*, trans. Saralyn R. Daly.

Pantheon Books for "The Wolf and the Three Girls" and "Uncle Wolf" from Italo Calvino, *Italian Folktales*, trans. George Martin.

HarperCollins for "The Spider in the Keyhole," "The Flea and the Sheep," "The Falcon and the Duck" from *The Fables of Leonardo da Vinci*, trans. Bruno Nardini.

"Coyote and Spider" and "Coyote Imitates Mountain Lion" from Barry Holstun Lopez, copyright © 1977. Reprinted by permission of Andrews McMeel Publishing. All rights reserved.

Saros International Publishers for "The Promise" and "Crime and Punishment" from Ken Saro-Wiwa, *The Singing Anthill: Ogoni Folk Tales*.

Victor Montejo for "The Rabbit and the Goat," and for "The Snail and the Minnow," "The War of the Wasps," and "The King of the Animals," from *The Bird Who Cleans the World and Other Mayan Fables*. Curbstone Press, 1991.

Carla Muschio for "Da dove vengono i bambini?" ("Where Do Children Come From?")

Third World Press for Nubia Kai, "Why the Spider Brings Money," and *The Sweetest Berry on the Bush* (1993).

Exposition Press for "How Spider Paid His Debts" and "The Spider and the Fox" from *Ghana Folk Tales: Ananse Stories from Africa*.

*For children
and
grandchildren, everywhere*

Contents

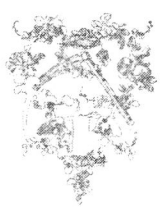

Introduction ix
    Fable as Genre x
    Fable Collections xvii

Panchatantra 1
    The Mice Who Set the Elephants Free 2
    Spot's Captivity 6
    Loss of Gains 12
    The Monkey and the Crocodile 12
    The Four Treasure Seekers 17

Jataka Tales 24
    The Golden Deer 24
    The Monkey and the Crocodile 28

Aesopic Fables, *by Phaedrus* 32
    The Vain Jackdaw 33
    The Fox and the Grapes 33
    The Fox and the Crow 33
    The Wolf and the Lamb 34
    The Peacock and the Crane 34
    The Lion and the Mouse 34
    The Oak and the Reeds 35
    The Frogs Asking for a King 35
    The Hare and the Tortoise 35
    Town Mouse and Country Mouse 36
    The Lion and the Bull 36

Kalila and Dimna 37
    The Monkey and the Tortoise 37

Fables, *by Marie de France* 41
    Prologue 41
    The Wolf and the Lamb 42
    The Crow and the Fox 43

    The Lion and the Mouse 44
    The Crow in Peacock's Feathers 45
    The Beetle 46
    Epilogue 47

The Book of Good Love, *by Juan Ruiz* 49
    The Fable of the Dog That Was Carrying a Piece of Meat
       in His Mouth 49
    The Fable of the Lion Who Killed Himself in Anger 50

Mathnawi, *by Rumi* 51
    The Unseen Elephant 51

Fables, *by Leonardo da Vinci* 52
    The Spider in the Keyhole 52
    The Flea and the Sheep 53
    The Falcon and the Duck 53

Fables, *by Jean de la Fontaine* 55
    The Grasshopper and the Ant 56
    The Raven and the Fox 57
    The Wolf and the Lamb 57
    Death and the Woodcutter 58
    The Oak and the Reed 59
    The Frogs Who Asked for a King 60
    The Animals Sick of the Plague 61
    The Power of Fables 62
    The Rat and the Elephant 64
    The Hare and the Frogs 65
    The Two Pigeons 66
    The Owl and the Mice 68

Mother Goose Tales, *by Charles Perrault* 70
    Little Red Riding-Hood 70

Fable of the Bees, *by Bernard Mandeville* 73
    The Moral 73

Fables and Epigrams, *by G.E. Lessing* 75
    The Raven and the Fox 75
    The Man and the Dog 76
    The Sick Wolf 76

Fables, *by Ivan Krylov* 77
    The Wolf in the Kennel 77

  Pike and Cat 78
  Eagle and Spider... 78
  The Ant 79
  The Wolves and the Sheep 80

Uncle Remus, *by Joel Chandler Harris* 81
  Uncle Remus Initiates the Little Boy 81

Cric? Crac!/Fables Créoles, *by Georges Sylvain* 85
  Crow and Fox 85

The Bird Who Cleans the World and Other
  Mayan Fables, *by Victor Montejo*.. 88
  The Snail and the Minnow 88
  The War of the Wasps 88
  The King of the Animals 90
  The Rabbit and the Goat (short version) 91

Native North American Fables, *by Barry Lopez*........................ 96
  Coyote and Spider 96
  Coyote Imitates Mountain Lion 97

The Sweetest Berry on the Bush, *by Nubia Kai* 98
  Why the Spider Brings Money 98

Chinese Fables 100
  The Orangutans 100
  Vegetarian Cat 101
  Yang Bu Beats His Dog 102
  The Owl Moves House 103
  Killing His Father by Hitting a Fly 104
  A Hen and a Crow 105
  The Wolf and the Lamb, *by Ying Wu* 102

Fables, *by Leo Tolstoy*.. 105
  The Wolf and the Old Woman 105
  The Falcon and the Cock 105
  The Gnat and the Lion 106
  The Hedgehog and the Hare 106

An Aesop Fable, *by Leon Trotsky* 108

Peace Among the Beasts, *by Colette* 109
  The Bear and the Old Lady 109

Fables for Our Time, *by James Thurber*..................................... 113
  The Elephant Who Challenged the World 113

Further Fables for Our Time "Variations on a Theme" 115
    I 115
    II 115
    III 115
    IV 116

Italian Folk Tales, *by Italo Calvino* 117
    The Wolf and the Three Girls 117
    Uncle Wolf 118

Where Do Children Come From?, *by Carla Muschio* 121

Hottentot Fables 125
    The Tortoises Hunting the Ostriches 125
    The Giraffe and the Tortoise 125
    Which Was the Thief? 126
    The Lion and the Baboon 126

Ananse Stories From Ghana 129
    How the Spider Paid His Debts 129
    The Spider and the Fox 129

Ogoni Folk Tales, *by Ken Saro-Wiwa* 131
    Crime and Punishment 131
    The Promise 134

Bibliography *139*

Introduction

An ancient form of literary composition, fables are one of the few literary genres that exist in one form or another all over the world. As such, they remind us that people everywhere may indeed have more in common than is often assumed. As fictitious, short, secular narratives often using animal figures to convey a truth, fables invariably draw attention to typical human behavior or to human traits that are drawn out or exaggerated in particular situations. Fables are also a literary means to engage in political, philosophical, and ethical speculation outside the realm of absolute moral and religious convictions.

We could refer to the fable as a kind of metaphor, for the story shows us that the animal characters in the narrative behave like humans. The conventions of the fable require that the traits of animals be fixed, so that as metaphors, they can convey what they represent transparently. Thus, the wolf, like the crocodile, is a predator and therefore dangerous. Mice, hares, tortoises, sheep, monkeys, and deer, because they are the victims of the predatory animals, become vulnerable and weak in the natural order. As such, they must use various talents to avoid the ravenous appetites of the larger animals. Every creature has an environmental niche in a natural order that is biologically determined. The fable depends on the simple recognition that animals such as lions, elephants, crocodiles, and wolves possess greater physical power in the natural order whereas mice, deer, hares, and sheep face the constant threat of attacks from larger and usually predatory animals. But despite their natural weakness, the powerless animals often have unique traits that permit them to survive in the face of threats from the stronger beasts. Also, creatures such as wasps, spiders, termites, and hornets, though tiny, alone or massed together, have the power to resist, undermine, or even destroy the most powerful of animals. Although the specific animals differ depending on the geographic origin of the fable, the divisions between large, vulnerable, crafty, cunning, predatory, regal, slow, fast, proud, humble, etc. are pervasive throughout the traditional world of fables.

Frequently proverbial, without fostering absolute moral or ethical principles, the fable usually offers conventional worldly wisdom. It provides advice for survival in a tricky world where the weak are vulnerable to the superior strength and capriciousness of the powerful. The "truth" the fable expresses is tentative or situational; one could say a particular truth fits a particular circumstance. In this respect, the fable's contingent teachings contrast radically with those of myth, whose principles or "truths" are often considered absolute. Myths or sacred narratives frequently enunciate central codes or laws by which a group of people sustains itself as a community. The Exodus narrative in the Hebrew Bible, the *Mahabharata*, or the *Aeneid* offer examples of this feature of myth, for at critical moments in these epics, the absolute laws by which the people define themselves are proclaimed.

Fable as Genre

"Every poetic expression with which a writer wishes to convey a moral point of view is a fable," writes the German philosopher G. E. Lessing.[1] This purely formal, aesthetic definition applies, of course, to almost any imaginative discourse. What makes fable distinct is that as a narrative form featuring animal characters, it nearly always contains a moral or lesson, or the narrative as metaphor is itself intended to convey a moral. This split structure situates the fable midway between the wisdom of the proverb or aphorism, on the one hand, and the magical plot of the fairy tale, on the other. From a semiological point of view, what the fable represents, in the words of Fredric Jameson is "the tendency of the narrative material to split in two and to go in two different verbal or semiotic directions—on the one hand, into narrative proper, an anecdote, in which either human or animal characters are shown doing something with certain results or outcomes; and a relatively more abstract lesson (or 'moral' to use the technical term) is juxtaposed with the preceding narrative and offered as the latter's meaning or 'lesson.' "[2] Although many fairy tales do generate morals, these often appear like aphorisms grafted onto a story that has been retold to emphasize contemporary social issues. Fables, on the other hand, are the genre that deliberately features the connection between narrative and proverb.

In this hybrid situation, fables most closely resemble parables, which likewise offer a narrative embodiment of some higher truth. In the parable, however, the lesson to be drawn remains implicit though regulated by a determined code of interpretation. Because traditional parables (as opposed to literary ones written by modern authors like Franz Kafka or Jorge Luis Borges) are told in the context of religious truths, these truths function as the code through which the parable can be understood or interpreted, as for example the parables of Jesus in the New Testament gospels. The speaker, Jesus, and the truths understood as proclaimed by the gospels become the means by which to interpret the parables. But unlike the theoretical or even transcendental wisdom a reader is expected to draw from the religious parable, the lowly fable proposes a practical and overall secular sense that puts its roots in popular and peasant culture. Here, too, we may note a difference in register between the earthy familiarity of the animals in fables and the marvelous or monstrous beasts of fairy tales.

Fables are among the most widespread of narrative forms, appearing in virtually every culture and historical period. The two most disseminated and celebrated traditions are those from ancient India (Bidpai) and Greece (Aesopian). The very prevalence of the form does not exclude, however, the widest possible set of opinions about its meanings, reception, and significance. It has been dismissed as children's literature, espoused as the epitome of folk wisdom, used as a pedagogical tool in European schoolbooks from the Middle Ages to the 19th century, and even taken as revolutionary allegory of social and political inequities. Fables are dismissed for being so manifestly implausible (beasts that talk, etc.) yet lauded for exposing some hidden truth in the guise of a fantasy.

In fact, however, despite Lessing's and Jean de La Fontaine's claim for the unity of narrative and lesson, the dichotomy that defines the genre is also the key to its interpretive variability: "But it is easy to see that the Aesop fable in its present form of 'fabula docet' (story teaches) makes its presentation either simple or heavy as a punch in the face, so that often the opposite to its moral or a better version of the moral can be derived."[3] In other words, the moral—especially in its more "heavy-handed" manifestations—is frequently at odds with the story line, which may imply a different or even contrary lesson.

Like the sacred text, the fable calls for a figural interpretation of its literal content, but unlike scripture or parable, the possible layers of interpretation remain indeterminate because they are not constrained by the context of canon, gospel, doctrine, or other restricting means applied in biblical or other religious hermeneutics. Understanding a fable is above all an exercise in reading, of drawing a lesson from the anthropomorphized natural world where the marvelous is curiously presented as quotidian. Indeed this incongruity between the strange and the prosaic is what cries out for an interpretive moral that will justify the obvious implausibility of the tale by the truth of the moral. Lessing correctly points out that the non-wondrous and indeed stereotypical familiarity of the animals in fables is key to the genre's representational economy. But the relation of story and moral obliges the reader to interpret the narrative, either in accordance with its explicitly stated lesson or possibly at odds with it. For example, we have the French plebian Rousseau's scandalized explication in *Emile* of the fable about "The Crow and the Fox," where he discovers the fable not to be teaching the dangers of vanity (from the vantage point of the crow) but the value of deceit (the fox's point of view).[4] One could just as well translate this opposition into the necessary difference in life strategies between the "haves" and the "have nots," i.e. those whose vanity dovetails with their having something to lose and those who must resort to ruse in order to survive. Interestingly, Lessing himself rewrites this fable to prevent such a revisionist understanding by having the crow hold poisoned meat in its beak rather than cheese. It is the fox who is punished for his deceitful flattery, then, and dies from eating the bad meat.

For Hegel, the 19th-century German philosopher, the prosaic quality of the fable is precisely where it reveals its social roots and therefore its inferiority as an aesthetic genre: "still its ideas are merely clever, without the energy of the Spirit or the insight in substantive vision, without poetry and philosophy. Its perspective and teachings turn out to be witty and clever, but it remains delving into the trivial . . . because its moral can't be openly stated, but is merely hidden, like in a riddle that is understood when it is solved. Prose begins with slaves and so the genre is prosaic" (I: 376). According to Hegel's materialist approach, the fable is a genre that speaks indirectly of the desires, fantasies, and utopian aspirations of the oppressed while denouncing the brutality of rapacious elites who prey on the disempowered in a manner analogous to the unmerciful beasts portrayed in fables. In the vision of the oppressed, the world is indeed a jungle or forest full of perils for the unsuspecting, a place ruled by brute force and where only trickery and wit can save one from becoming just another victim—hence, the common cautionary themes of fables about the dangers of dealing with the powerful when the weak are unable to turn the tables against them. The legendary representation of the character of Aesop himself dramatizes this voice of the alien or outcaste speaking through the fable. Tradition has held that Aesop was a social and racial "other," an eloquent slave reputedly of either Phrygian or Ethiopian origin, who was physically deformed to the point of approximating beastliness as well, yet whose storytelling wit earned him freedom and fame. In a strong sense, the world of the fable is that of oral and popular tradition, the babbling realm before or outside academic and professional systems of writing that is associated with children, women, the illiterate, and the mad. This populist understanding of the fable is the one that prevails among modern critics of the genre.[5]

Caution should be taken, however, before applying this methodological point of view uncritically to the *written* archive of fables (Steinhöwel, Caxton, La Fontaine, et al.), especially given the literary reception and pedagogical application of such anthologies as texts proper for the moral edification of school children. The creation of a canon of fables at the beginning of modern capitalist society also heightened the contradiction between story and lesson. La Fontaine's poetic rendering of Aesop's fables, for instance, later became a pillar of the French education system. Middle-class morality and the development of a bourgeois democratic society in 19th-century France combined to obscure La Fontaine's subversive political motivations, which had led to his disgrace and exile at the dawn of Louis XIV's reign. Instead of a cynical critique of power relations, La Fontaine's fables came to exemplify social virtues such as thrift, loyalty, and hard work.

Such contradictory possibilities are what make the fable so explosively applicable to political and historical change while ultimately making its ideological convictions elusive. While the legend of Aesop as originator of the genre has long since been discounted, speculation remains that a historical figure like him would have achieved notoriety not by inventing the fable itself but by developing a new *use* of it as critique and satire of the new political landscape under the Greek tyrants. The legendary figure of Aesop eventually paid with his life for this creative spin on the genre, which despite its hidden messages eventually had to antagonize the elites against which the fables were directed.

The subsequent history of the fable as political allegory is a rich one, perhaps reaching high tide with Machiavelli's fox/lion analogy in *The Prince,* Hobbes' development of the man/wolf analogy in *Leviathan,* and Mandeville's compendious *Fable of the Bees.*[6] With Mandeville, the fable turns from the representation of political ills and/or moral virtues to the philosophical exploration of social relations themselves. First published in 1705 as a short pamphlet containing a poem, "The Grumbling Hive," with the paradoxical moral that "private vices" have "publick benefits," *The Fable of the Bees* grew in the course of its many editions over the next 28 years to the monumental, two-volume opus it is, as Mandeville added various "remarks," essays, a "vindication of the book," and a series of dialogues all in response to the savage polemics aroused by the fable. The contradiction between story and lesson could hardly be made more manifest, especially when aggravated by a moral that is itself paradoxical: Mandeville can be read either as a cynical apologist for the capitalist exploitation of labor power (anticipating Adam Smith and the liberalist economics of *laissez-faire*) or as its most disillusioned critic. On the one hand, the claim that private greed and self-interest may have social benefits would appear to justify any kind of exploitive behavior on the part of the privileged few. On the other hand, that same unjust behavior does not need to be morally exonerated for it to be acknowledged as a structural necessity that makes resistance to it pointless or at least highly problematic. In any case, Mandeville's influence on the subsequent development of economic theory is well known (including that fundamental concept of the division of labor) and reaches all the way to Karl Marx.

It is out of this tradition that we see Marx's satirical use of fables in the *18th Brumaire* as an instrument of political analysis, or their explanatory possibilities pursued in the analyses of capital. The fable, better known as that of "The Belly and the Members," is traditionally ascribed to the Roman patrician named Agrippa who would have declaimed it to quell a plebian rebellion by depicting the elite in a corporeal analogy with the stomach, which if not properly fed by the subservient limbs would in turn starve the latter. In a passage from *Das Kapital*, Marx turns the fable around from its bourgeois interpretation to denounce the very atomization not only of the body politic but also of the individual worker's body under the oppressive conditions of emerging industrial capitalism. In *Value, Price, and Profit*, the same fable is used counter to its traditional lesson of social loyalty to argue instead the efficacy of collective action against capitalist exploitation: "Agrippa failed to show that you feed the members of one man by filling the belly of an other."[7] In contrast to this revisionist use of particular fables to develop critical analogies, we also find the term fable or fabling used to designate the patent falsehoods by which capital obscures its material basis for social control and production. The fable is thus itself deployed in Marx both as a critical tool of Marxist science *and* as the very exemplum of ideology in action. Lenin and Trotsky, in particular, are also able practitioners of fabling in this sense, and their works are full both with admiring allusions to the folk wisdom of particular fables and with denunciations of various forms of ideological aberration, calumny, and opportunism as mere fables.

In the contemporary world, we see the continued ideological manipulation of children through fable in their mass-media derivations pioneered by Disney and imitated by countless others. In place of the "hard" lessons offered by the animal characters in classic fables—where any lapse of judgment could mean becoming someone else's meal—the likes of Mickey Mouse and Scoobydoo propose only cuteness, silliness and what, from the perspective of traditional fable, could only be a dangerous foolishness presenting itself as anodyne insipidity. Even more cynical are the campaigns of corporate advertisers targeting children as malleable consumers. Nevertheless, new media also give new opportunities for countering such hegemonic and popular cultural expression. On the one hand, we see in the tradition of Joel Chandler Harris a renewed effort to collect, augment and disseminate subaltern fable traditions, such as those put together by Georges Sylvain,[8] J.-M. Awouma,[9] William Saroyan[10] and Victor Montejo[11] of, respectively Haitian, Camerounian, Armenian, and Mayan Fables. And on the other hand, we find the simultaneously ironic and pedagogic appropriation of the fable form by dissident movements. Don Durito, the jungle beetle, created by Subcomandante Insurgente Marcos of the Zapatista Liberation Army, has become a veritable icon of postcolonial resistance, disseminated as his texts and images have been by fax and internet as well as by print. In ironic allusion to Don Quixote, Durito tilts at the windmills of state terror and multinational corporatism with his paperclip lance riding atop his trusty steed, "Pegasus," who is in actuality a lowly turtle. In the course of his humorous adventures, however, Durito offers trenchant lessons on the power ruses and perils of contemporary neoliberal economics, not only as it affects Chiapas but the rest of the world. At the same time, and in accordance with the fable's traditional deployment of animal characters as humans in disguise, Durito the bug also puts a human face on those whom state terror (here, that of Mexico) would deny any semblance of humanity and who therefore appear only in masked guise. As such, Durito functions as an emblem of the critical potential of the fable, even or especially in a postmodern climate of irony and cynicism. That potential comes from the ability of this formally dialectical genre to adapt itself to differing socio-historical contexts and to speak the story of those who hear it.[12]

Mention must also be made of the philosophical commonplace of the world as a fable (*mundus est fabula*) that dates back at least as far as the pre-Socratic contemporaries of Aesop and reaches its culmination in modern philosophers like Nietzsche and Heidegger and in various forms of postmodernism. These approaches cast doubt on the possibility of any certain knowledge beyond its literary and linguistic expression. But if knowledge can never be more than an edifying story, if science itself is myth, then the only truth would be in a discourse that announces its own expression as fiction—fable in the etymological sense of a talking, Latin *fari* from Sanskrit *bha*. In other words, the moral of the fable would be then nothing more than the story itself and the pleasure of its retelling.

On the other hand, fabling can be understood less abstractly as being in a constant relation of symbolic possibility to what it recounts, as being in an allegorical relation to its referent, something first theorized by Fontenelle in "De l'origine des fables," ("Of the Origin of Fables") where he sees the fable not only as the earliest form of history but also as "the history of the errors of the human spirit."[13] This *history* of human errors is indeed what fables both disclose and propagate, urging us to read their testimony of what Walter Benjamin called the "catastrophe" of history[14] in their seemingly childlike narration of the unforgiving power relations between beasts that are all too human.

Fable Collections

Fables can form part of an oral repertoire of wisdom literature or they can appear in written compositions. But they flow back and forth between what we might call "oral style," a traditional mode of storytelling passed on through the ages, and literary style. They originated in communities without writing or where writing was not important and continue to exist as oral recitations even today, but they also originate in books, as the work of self-conscious literary artists. Traditional oral narratives were and continue to be recorded and written as they are orally recited. Fables also have been collected and arranged by compilers from oral or written resources into written form. As written forms, they thrived in the ancient and medieval periods, from India to Europe, having been collected as early as the fifth century B.C.E. Our oldest collections include the Indian *Panchatantra*,[15] Jataka tales,[16] and the *Hitopadesa*,[17] as well as the Greek and Latin collections of Aesopic material in Phaedrus and Babrius. The medieval period inherited the Indian collections as they traveled from East to West through Persian and Arabic. *The Case of the Animals versus Man Before the King of the Jinn*, a tenth century ecological fable produced by the pluralist Islamic Pure Brethren of Basra[18] in Iraq, is one of the most brilliant fables of this period. It uses the genre to launch a complex philosophical and anthropological inquiry into what distinguishes humans from the rest of the zoological world. The discussion follows after the animals, justifiably, accuse humans of having enslaved them. Modern in its understanding of ecological niches and evolutionary adaptation, the animals' argument resembles modern environmental positions that see animals as victims of human rapacity that endangers the survival of the natural world.

The tales of Kalila and Dimna (see introductions to selections in this collection), translated from Sanskrit to Pahlavi, then to Arabic, arrived in Iberia in the 11th or 12th century. Another classic of the medieval period, Petrus Alfonsi's *Disciplina Clericalis* (*The Scholar's Guide*),[19] was written by a Jewish convert to Christianity in Iberia in the 12th century. Like the work of the Brethren of Basra and *Kalila and Dimna*, it reflects the religious pluralism of that period in Iberia as it debates ethical issues in the context of a multicultural social environment.

These collections of fables, often transformed from their oral or other literary setting, can also be incorporated into later collections and literary frames for aesthetic or other cultural purposes. This is precisely what happened, for example, with the *Panchatantra* and *Fables of Bidpai: Kalila and Dimna*,[20] which became sources for Juan Ruiz, a 14th-century Castilian writer[21] and for La Fontaine.[22]

The Panchatantra, one of the oldest written collections of fables in the world is an example of how fables, originating in an oral environment, can become part of a literary tradition that then moves on from its indigenous setting. As an oral work, it dates to ancient Indian tradition, but it reached a written composed and collected form in Sanskrit in the early centuries of the first millennium. It was very popular and eventually was translated into Pahlavi, 531–79 C.E.; Syriac, 570; Persian and Arabic in the middle of the 8th century C.E., Greek, and Hebrew by the 13th century. The Arabic version, usually translated *Kalila and Dimna*, the Arabic names of the two main characters in the first collection of tales (*Loss of Friends*), was the source for all the European versions. The first of these was in Latin, followed by Spanish, German, French, and English among others. *The Panchatantra* is a *niti-shastra*, that is, a collection of advice for the wise conduct of life. It is not a specifically religious or moral work, suggesting that it was not produced by or for the priestly or learned class, but emerged as popular practical wisdom.

Fables based on the Latin Aesopic tradition are generally regarded as separate from the Indian tradition until the Middle Ages when, due to the Arabic translations and the Arabic civilization of Iberia, the two traditions began to merge. They were so important to European medieval education that the genre was transformed. The short narrative forms, typical of Phaedrus, the Latin preserver of the Aesopic tradition, were developed into expansive beast fables, like the French *Roman de Renart*,[23] a beast epic about the wiliness of a fox, or Geoffrey Chaucer's "Nun's Priest's Tale."[24] Both, like the medieval Sephardim Hebrew *Fox Fables* of Rabbi Berechiah Ha-Nakdan,[25] are satirical exposés of the powerful in the world of the Church and the feudal social structure. From this period onward, the genre has been consciously adopted for parodic and satiric purposes. This has resulted in collections like Leonardo da Vinci's *Fables*[26] or Jean de La Fontaine's rewriting of the fables from the ancient traditions of India, Greece, and Persia, and the adaptation of Latin, French, and Italian versions of the Aesopic materials. In turn, modern writers, like George Orwell in *Animal Farm*[27] or Salman Rushdie in *Haroun and the Sea of Stories*,[28] have adopted the traits and features of the fable genre to launch complex political and social commentaries on our times.

Though the fable itself is "a fictitious story picturing a truth" as defined by the ancient Greek rhetorician Theon in his *Progymnasmata,* the collecting of fables proves to have more varied purposes. Clearly a tradition that goes back to ancient times, as testified by the Jataka tales and by the *Panchatantra,* the diverse purposes of the compilations demonstrate the plasticity of the genre itself. The collections can reflect biases, depending on the compiler and the rationale for the compilation. The collections of tales that include different versions of the same story-type point to the various purposes to which the genre may be assigned. For example, in some missionary collections of traditional African fables in the 19th century, a title like *Reynard the Fox in South Africa or Hottentot Fables and Tales* is an effort, as the writer puts it, to show "that their [the Hottentots'] literary activity has been employed almost in the same direction as that which has been taken in our own earliest literature."[29]

When Italo Calvino selected and retold the folktales of his native Italy, collected in *Italian Folktales*[30] in the 1950s, he saw his efforts as very different from those of earlier compilers like the Grimm brothers. The Grimms believed they were salvaging the ancient German narratives to create a national consciousness in Germany.[31] By contrast, Calvino became obsessed with compiling the infinite variety and repetition of the folktale genre. But, though he seemed to shun the Grimms' intentions, calling his effort "hybrid," he nonetheless was committed, as he wrote, to present "every type of folktale, the existence of which is documented in Italian dialects; and the representation of all regions of Italy."[32] His effort was deeply invested in the variety and complexity of the Italian dialects and traditional story-telling arts as they still existed in the regions of Italy in the 1950s.

With the great tragedy of the rapid disappearance of indigenous cultures predicted by Claude Levi-Strauss in *Tristes Tropiques*[33] as one of the legacies of the 20th century, compilers have striven to record and translate the traditional stories of these people. But now the compiler strives to retain the identity of a people by inscribing their narratives for audiences far removed their origins. Thus Victor Montejo remembers his Mayan grandmother's fables and rewrites them to remember and recall her world. Ken Sara-Wiwa, who was executed by the Nigerian government in 1995 for protesting the multinational oil companies' destruction of his Ogoni people's indigenous lands, is another example of this contemporary phenomenon. In the introduction to his collection of tales, *The Singing Anthill: Ogoni Folk Tales*, published in 1991, he wrote: "The pre-literate society from which these tales emanate is certainly gone; the Ogoni still fish and farm but their lives are ringed around today, not by spirits but by oil wells and gas flares, and the harsh crudity of Nigerian politics which threatens their very survival as a people."[34] Thus, we can see that from the *Panchatantra* to *Ogoni Folk Tales*, the collecting of fables reflects an enduring investment in the fable as a means to debate ethical, social, political, and cultural values. The positions adopted may be useful and entertaining, as well as controversial and even subversive, but like the narratives that convey them, they continue to reside in the secular domain where advice and answers remain contextual and provisional.

1. Gotthold Ephraim Lessing, *Fabeln und Fabelabhandlungen, Werke und Briefe*, hgg. W. Barner et al (Frankfurt: Deutscher Klassiker Verlag, 1997), b. IV, 345. *Fables and Epigrams* (London: Applegath, 1825).
2. Fredric Jameson, *Brecht and Method* (Durham, N.C.: Duke University Press, 1998), 186.
3. Georg Wilhelm Friedrich Hegel, *Asthetik*, ed. Georg Lukács (Frankfurt: Europäische Verlagsanstalt, 1965), I, 374.
4. Jean-Jacques Rousseau, *Emile, ou de l'éducation, Oeuvres complètes*, v. 4, ed. Bernard Gagnebin and Marcel Raymond (Paris: Gallimard, 1959–1995).
5. Annabel Patterson, *Fables of Power: Aesopian Writing and Political History* (Durham, N.C.: Duke University Press, 1991) and Louis Marin, *Le récit est un piège* (Paris: Éditions de Minuit, 1978); L. Marin, *La parole mangée et autres essais théologico-politiques* (Paris: Klincksieck, 1986); Michel de Certeau, *La fable mystique* (Paris: Gallimard, 1982).
6. Bernard Mandeville, *Fable of the Bees: Private Vices, Publick Benefits* (Oxford: F. B. Kaye, 1924).
7. *Marx-Engels Gesamtausgabe* (Berlin/Moscow: Institut für Marxismus-Leninismus beim ZK der KPsSU and Institut für Marxismus-Leninismus beim ZK der SED, 1975–1989; since 1992, Berlin/Amsterdam: Internationalen Marx-Engels-Stiftung Amsterdam), I:20:148.
8. Georges Sylvain, *Cric? Crac!: fables créoles* (Haiti: Éditions Fardin, 1901).
9. Joseph Marie Awouma, *Contes et fables du Cameroun: Initiation à la littérature orale* (Yaoundé: Éditions Clé, 1976).
10. William Saroyan, *Saroyan's Fables* (New York: Harcourt Brace, 1941).
11. Victor Montejo, *The Bird Who Cleans the World and Other Mayan Fables* (Willimantic, Conn.: Curbstone Press, 1991).
12. Subcomandante Marcos, *Shadows of Tender Fury: The Letters and Communiqués of Subcomandante Marcos and the Zapatista Army of National Liberation* (New

York: 1995); Subcomandante Marcos, *Tales of Durito*, gopher://mundo.eco.utexas.edu:70m/1m/mailing/chiapas95.archive/EZLN%Communiques/Tales%20of%Durito.
13. Bernard de Fontenelle, "De l'origine des fables," *Oeuvres* (Paris, 1790), 372.
14. Walter Benjamin, *Illuminations*, ed. and introd. Hannah Arendt and trans. Harry Zohn (New York: Harcourt Brace, 1968), 257.
15. *The Panchatantra*, trans. Arthur W. Ryder (Chicago: University of Chicago Press, 1925).
16. *The Hungry Tigress: Buddhist Legends and Jataka Tales*, versions of Rafe Martin (Berkeley, Calif.: Parallax Press, 1990).
17. *Animal Fables of India: Narayana's Hitopadesha or Friendly Counsel*, trans. Francis G. Hutchins (West Franklin, N.H.: Amarta Press, 1985).
18. *The Case of the Animals versus Man Before the King of the Jinn*, trans. from Arabic with intro. and commentary Lenn Evan Goodman (Boston: Twayne, 1978).
19. Pedro Alfonso, *The Scholar's Guide*, trans. Joseph Ramon Jones and John Esten Keller (Toronto: Pontifical Institute of Medieval Studies, 1969).
20. *Kalila and Dimna: Selected Fables of Bidpai*, retold by Ramsay Wood with an introduction by Doris Lessing (London: Granada, 1980).
21. Juan Ruiz, *The Book of Good Love*, trans. Saralyn R. Daly (University Park, Penn.: Pennsylvania State University Press, 1978).
22. Jean de La Fontaine, *Fables choisies mises en vers* (Paris: 1668).
23. *Renard the Fox: The Adventures of an Epic Hero*, trans. Patricia Terry (Berkeley, Calif.: University of California Press, 1992).
24. *The Canterbury Tales* in *The Riverside Chaucer*, ed. Larry D. Benson (Boston: Houghton Mifflin, 1987).
25. *Fables of a Jewish Aesop*, trans. from *Fox Fables of Berechiah ha-Nakdan* (New York: Columbia University Press, 1967).
26. *The Fables of Leonardo da Vinci*, trans. Bruno Nardini (New York: HarperCollins, 1973).
27. George Orwell, *Animal Farm* (New York: Harcourt Brace, 1946).
28. Salman Rushdie, *Haroun and the Sea of Stories* (London: Viking, 1990).
29. W. H. I. Bleek, *Reynard the Fox in South Africa or Hottentot Fables and Tales* (London: Trübner, 1864), xii-xiii.
30. Italo Calvino, *Italian Folktales*, trans. George Martin (New York: Pantheon, 1956).
31. Jacob and Wilhelm Grimm, *Deutsches Wörterbuch* (Leipzig: S. Hirzel, 1854).
32. Calvino, *Italian Folktales*, xx.
33. Claude Levi-Strauss, *Tristes Tropiques* (Paris: Plon, 1955).
34. Ken Saro-Wiwa, *The Singing Anthill: Ogoni Folk Tales* (London and Lagos: Saros International Publishers, 1991), 10.

Panchatantra

The Panchatantra is the oldest known "framed" narrative in the world. As an oral work, it dates to ancient Indian tradition, but it reached a written composed and collected form in Sanskrit, an ancient Indian literary language, by the sixth century C.E. or earlier. It was very popular and eventually was translated into Pahlavi, 531–579 C.E., Syriac, 570, Persian, and Arabic in the middle of the eighth century C.E., and Hebrew by the thirteenth century. The Arabic version, usually translated *Kalila and Dimna*, the Arabic names of the two main characters in the first collection of tales (*Loss of Friends*), was the source for all the European versions. The first of these was in Latin, followed by Spanish, German, French, and English among others. Tradition has held that a person named Vishnu Sharman, whose name appears in the text, was responsible for the collection, but little is known about him. *The Panchatantra* is a *niti-shastra*, that is, a collection of advice for the wise conduct of life. It is not a specifically religious or moral work, but a series of fables designed to provide practical wisdom.

A framed narrative is a collection of stories that is held together by a larger frame story. The frame narrative for the *Panchatantra* is as follows: A king named Amara Shakti had three sons who were unwilling to learn anything. The king, full of despair over the future of his realm with such sons as heirs, engaged Vishnu Sharman, a Brahman teacher, who set about educating the boys in practical wisdom. Unwilling to accept any payment, the teacher devised a series of stories arranged in five books, each of which also has a frame, that would teach the princes. These are titled *Loss of Friends; Winning Friends; Crows and Owls; Loss of Gains;* and *Ill-Considered Action*. The following selections are taken from *Winning Friends, Loss of Gains*, and *Ill-Considered Action*. In the *Panchatantra*, the basic fable story is told in prose but verses provide the practical wisdom in proverbs and teachings, so this more elaborate form of the fable becomes a hybrid between verse and prose.

The Mice Who Set the Elephants Free

This excerpt is from Winning Friends, *in which the central narrative tells the story of four animal friends, Spot, the deer; Swift, the crow; Gold, the mouse; and Slow, the turtle, who retreat to the forest. Told by Spot, the deer, the tale follows the verse,* "Make friends, make friends, however strong/ Or weak they be:/ Recall the captive elephants/ That mice set free," *and recommends the advantages of friendship across the natural boundaries of powerful and powerless.*

There was once a region where people, houses, and temples had fallen into decay. So the mice, who were old settlers there, occupied the chinks in the floors of stately dwellings with sons, grandsons (both in the male and female line), and further descendants as they were born, until their holes formed a dense tangle. They found uncommon happiness in a variety of festivals, dramatic performances (with plots of their own invention), wedding feasts, eating parties, drinking bouts, and similar diversions. And so the time passed.

But into this scene burst an elephant-king, whose retinue numbered thousands. He, with his herd, had started for the lake upon information that there was water there. As he marched through the mouse community, he crushed faces, eyes, heads, and necks of such mice as he encountered.

Then the survivors held a convention. "We are being killed," they said, "by these lumbering elephants—curse them! If they come this way again, there will not be mice enough for seed. Besides:

> An elephant will kill you, if
> He touch; a serpent if he sniff;
> King's laughter has a deadly sting;
> A rascal kills by honoring.

Therefore let us devise a remedy effective in this crisis." When they had done so, a certain number went to the lake, bowed before the elephant-king, and said respectfully: "O King, not far from here is our community, inherited from a long line of ancestors. There we have prospered through a long succession of sons and grandsons. Now you gentlemen, while coming here to water, have destroyed us by the thousands. Furthermore, if you travel that way again, there will not be enough of us for seed. If then you feel compassion toward us, pray travel another path. Consider the fact that even creatures of our size will some day prove of some service." And the elephant-king turned over in his mind what he had heard, decided that the statement of the mice was entirely logical, and granted their request. Now in the course of time a certain king commanded his elephant-trappers to trap elephants. And they constructed a so-called water-trap, caught the elephant-king with his herd, three days later dragged him out with a great tackle made of ropes and things, and tied him to stout trees in that very bit of forest. When the trappers had gone, the elephant-king reflected thus: "In what manner, or through whose assistance, shall I be delivered?" Then it occurred to him: "We have no means of deliverance except those mice."

So the king sent the mice an exact description of his disastrous position in the trap through one of his personal retinue, an elephant-cow who had not ventured into the trap, and who had previous information of the mouse community.

When the mice learned the matter, they gathered by the thousand, eager to return the favor shown them, and visited the elephant herd. And seeing king and herd fettered, they gnawed the guy-ropes where they stood, then swarmed up the branches, and by cutting the ropes aloft, set their friends free.

> And that is why I say:
> Make friends, make friends, however strong . . .
> and the rest of it.

[**Note:** As is the pattern in the *Panchatantra*, stories are embedded within the frame story of each book. At this point the central narrative of the second book, *The Winning of Friends,* resumes.]

When Slow had listened to this, he said: "Be it even so, my dear fellow. Have no fear. In this place you are at home. Pray dismiss anxieties and behave as in your own dwelling." So they all took food and recreation at such hours as suited each, met at the noon hour in the shade of crowding trees beside the broad lake, and spent their time in reciprocated friendship, discussing a variety of masterly works on religion, economics, and similar subjects. And this seems quite natural:

> For men of sense, good poetry
> And science will suffice:
> The time of dunderheads is spent
> In squabbling, sleep, and vice.

And again:

> A thrill
> Will fill
> The wisest heart,
> When flow
> Bons mots
> Composed with art
> Though fe-
> Males be
> Removed apart.

Now one day Spot failed to appear at the regular hour. And the others, missing him, alarmed also by an evil omen that appeared at that moment, drew the conclusion that he was in trouble, and could not keep up their spirits. Then Slow and Gold said to Swift: "Dear fellow, we two are prevented by locomotive limitations from hunting for our dear friend. We beg you, therefore, to hunt about and learn whether the poor fellow is eaten by a lion, or singed by forest fire, or fallen into the power of hunters and such creatures. There is a saying:

> One quickly fears for loved ones who
> In pleasure gardens play:
> What, then, if they in forests grim
> And peril-bristling stay.

By all means go, search out precise news concerning Spot, and return quickly. On hearing this, Swift flew a little distance to the edge of a swamp, and finding Spot caught in a stout trap braced with pegs of acacia-wood, he sorrowfully said: "My dear friend, how did you fall into this distress?"

"My friend," said Spot, "there is no time for delay. Listen to me.

> When life is near an end,
> The presence of a friend
> Brings happiness, allying
> The living with the dying.

Oh, pardon any expressions of friendly impatience I may have used in our discussions. Likewise, say to Gold and Slow in my name:

> If any ugly word
> Was willy-nilly heard,
> I pray you both, forgive—
> Let only friendship live.

On hearing this, Swift replied: "Feel no fear, my dear fellow, while you have friends like us. I will return with all speed, bringing Gold to cut your bonds."

Thereupon, his heart in a flutter, he found Slow and Gold, explained the nature of Spot's captivity, then returned to Spot, carrying Gold in his beak. Gold, for his part, on seeing the plight of his friend, sorrowfully said: "My dear fellow, you always had a wary mind and a shrewd eye. How, then, did you fall into this dreadful captivity?" And Spot rejoined: "Why ask, my friend? Fate, you know, does what it will. As the saying goes:

> What mortal flies
> (However wise)
> When billows rise
> To fatal size
> On seas of woe?

> In dead of night,
> Or broad daylight,
> Grim fate may smite;
> Ah, who can fight
> An unseen foe?

You, my saintly friend, are familiar with the caprices of constraining destiny. Therefore be quick. Cut my bonds before the pitiless hunter comes."

"Have no fear," said Gold, "while I am at your side. In my heart, however, is great sorrow, which I beg you to remove by telling your story. You are guided by an eye of wisdom. How did you fall into this captivity?"

"Well," said Spot, "if you insist on knowing, listen, and learn how I have been made captive a second time, having once before suffered the captivity."

"Tell me," said Gold, "how once before you suffered the woes of captivity. I am eager to learn the full detail." And Spot told the story of

[This is an example of how one story is halted while another is embedded.]

Spot's Captivity

Long ago, when I was six months old, I used to gambol in front of all the rest, as a youngster does. Out of sheer spirits I would run far ahead, then wait for the herd. Now we deer have two gaits, called the Jump-Up and the Straightaway. Of these I knew the Straightaway, but not the Jump-Up. While amusing myself one day, I lost touch with the herd. At this I was dreadfully worried, gazed about the horizon to learn where they might be, and discovered them ahead. Now they had avoided a snare by means of the Jump-Up; they stood in a body ahead of me, and waited, all looking at me. But I, ignorant of the Jump-Up, was caught in the hunter's snare. While I was trying to drag it toward the herd, the hunter bound all my limbs and I fell to the ground, head foremost. And the herd of deer vanished, seeing no hope of saving me.

When the hunter came up, he did not put me to death, for pity softened his heart at the thought: "He is a fawn, fit only for a pet." Instead, he carefully took me home and gave me as a plaything to a prince, who showed his delight at seeing me by giving the hunter a generous reward.

The prince treated me kindly, providing ointments, massage, baths, food, perfumes, and salves, while my meals were appropriate and palatable. But as I was passed from hand to hand by the curious women and princes at court, I was seriously inconvenienced by petting and scratching, which did not spare neck, eye, front hoof, hind hoof, or ear. Finally, one day in the rainy season, as the prince reclined on a couch, I observed the lightning, listened to the thunder, and, my heart wistful for my fondly remembered herd, I recited:

> When shall I follow on the herd
> Of coursing deer again?
> When brace myself against the wind
> That whistles by? Ah, when?

"Who said that?" cried the prince, and looked about him, terrified. When he saw me, he thought: "No man said it, but a deer. It is a prodigy. I am undone," and like one possessed by a devil, he tottered from the house, his garments in disarray.

Thinking himself ridden by a demon, he tempted the sorcerers and magicians with a great reward, saying: "If any free me from this torment, I will pay him no small honor." Meanwhile, overhasty individuals were striking me with sticks, bricks, and cudgels, but—further life being predestined—I was rescued by a certain holy man who said: "Why kill the poor beast?" Furthermore, he penetrated the cause of my malady, and respectfully said to the prince: "Dear sir, in the rainy season he wistfully remembered his native herd, and therefore recited:

> When shall I follow on the herd
> Of coursing deer again?
> When brace myself against the wind
> That whistles by? Ah, when?"

On hearing this, the prince was cured of his feverish malady, returned to his normal state, and said to his men: "Douse the poor deer's head in plenty of water, and set him free in the forest he came from." And they did so.

"Thus, though having suffered a previous captivity, I am caught again through constraining destiny."

At this moment Slow joined them. For his heart was so full of love for his friend that he had followed, leaving grass, shrubs, and speargrass crushed behind him. At sight of him, they were more distressed than ever, and Gold became their spokesman. "My dear fellow," said he, "you have done wrong in leaving your fortress to come here, since you are not able to save yourself from the hunter, while on us he cannot lay hands. For when the bonds are cut and the hunter stands near, Spot will bound away and disappear, Swift will fly into a tree, while I, being a little fellow, will find some chink to slide into. But what will you do, when within his reach?"

To this Slow listened, but he said: "Oh, do not blame me, you of all people. For

> The loss of love and loss of wealth
> Who could endure
> But for restoratives of health
> In friendship sure?

And again:

> The days when meetings do not fail
> With wise and good
> Are lovely clearings on the trail
> Through life's wild wood.
>
> The heart finds rest in telling things
> (When troubles toss)
> To honest wife, or friend who clings
> Or kindly boss.

Ah, my dear fellow,

> The wistful glances wander,
> The wits, bewildered, ponder
> In good men separated,
> Whose love is unabated.

And more than that:

> Better lose your life than friends;
> Life returns when this life ends,
> Not the sympathy that blends."

At this moment the hunter arrived, bow and arrow in hand. Under his very eyes Gold cut the bonds and slipped into the before-mentioned chink. Swift flew into the air and was gone. Spot darted away.

Now when the hunter saw that the deer's bonds had been cut, he was filled with amazement and said: "Under no circumstances do deer cut bonds. It was through fate that a deer has done it." Then he spied a turtle on most improbable terrain, and with mixed feelings he said: "Even if the deer, with fate's help, cut his bonds and escaped, still I've got this turtle. As the saying goes:

> Nothing comes, of all that walks,
> All that flies to heaven,
> All that courses o'er the earth,
> If it be not given."

After this meditation, the hunter cut spear-grass with his knife, wove a stout rope, tied the turtle's feet tightly together, fastened the rope to his bow-tip, and started home. But when Gold saw his friend borne away, he sorrowfully said: "Ah, me! Ah, me!

> No sooner sorrow's ocean-shore
> I reach in safety, than once more
> A bitter sorrow is my lot:
> Misfortunes crowd the weakest spot.

> Fresh blows are dreadful on a wound;
> Food fails, and hunger-pangs abound;
> Woes come, old enmities grow hot:
> Misfortunes crowd the weakest spot.

> One walks at ease on level ground
> Till one begins to stumble;
> Let stumbling start, and every step
> Is apt to bring a tumble.

And besides:

> It is hard to find in life
> A friend, a bow, a wife,
> Strong, supple to endure,
> In stock and sinew pure,
> In time of danger sure.

> False friends are common. Yes, but where
> True nature links a friendly pair,
> The blessing is as rich as rare.

> To bitter ends
> You trust true friends,
> Not wife nor mother,
> Not son nor brother.
>
> No long experience alloys
> True friendship's sweet and supple joys;
> No evil men can steal the treasure;
> It is death, death only, sets a measure.

"Ah, what is this fate that smites me ceaselessly. First came the loss of property; then humiliations from my own people, the result of poverty; because of gloom thereat, exile; and now fate prepares for me the loss of a friend. As the proverb says:

> In truth, I do not grieve though riches flee;
> Some lucky chance will bring them back to me:
> It is this that hurts me—lacking riches' stay,
> The best of friends relax and fall away.

And again:

> Fate's artful linkage since my birth
> Of evil deeds and deeds of worth
> Pursues me on this present earth
>
> Till states of mind that play and sway
> And change and range from day to day,
> Seem lives that strive and pass away.

Ah, there is only too much wisdom in this:

> The body, born, is near its doom;
> And riches are the source of gloom;
> All meetings end in partings: yes,
> The world is all one brittleness.

"Ah, me! Ah, me! The loss of my friend is death to me. What care I even for my own people? As the saying goes:

> A foe of woe and pain and fear,
> A cup of trust and feelings dear,
> A pearl—who made it? Who could blend
> Six letters in that name of friend?

Oh, friendly meetings!

> O joy to which the righteous cling,
> Machine that answers love's sole string,
> Pure happiness in every breath,
> Cut short by one stern exile—Death!

And once again:

> Pleasant riches; friendship's course
> In familiar ruts;
> Enmities of men of sense—
> Death abruptly cuts.

And one last word:

> If birth and death did not exist
> Nor age nor fear of loved ones missed,
> If all were not so quick to perish,
> Whose life were not a thing to cherish?"

While Gold recited these grief-stricken sentences, Spot and Swift joined him and united their lamentations with his. And Gold said to them: "So long as our dear Slow is within sight, so long we have a chance to save him. Leave us, Spot. You must slip past the troubled hunter unobserved, drop to earth somewhere near water, and pretend to be dead. Swift, you must spread your claws in the cagework of Spot's horns, pretend to peck out his eyes. Then that dreadful new beast of a hunter, in the greedy belief that he has found a dead deer, will certainly wish to seize him, will throw the turtle on the ground, and hurry up. When his back is turned, I for my part will in a mere twinkling set Slow free to seek refuge in the water nearby, his natural fortress. I myself will slide into a grass-clump. You, furthermore, must plan a second escape when the beast of a hunter is upon you." So they put this plan into practice.

Now when the hunter saw a deer as good as dead beside the water, and noticed that a crow was pecking at him, he joyfully threw the turtle on the ground and ran for a club. As soon as Spot could tell from the tramp of feet that the hunter was close upon him, with a supreme burst of speed he swept into dense forest. Swift flew into a tree. The turtle, his fettering cord cut by Gold, scrambled to shelter in the water. Gold slipped into a grass-clump. To the hunter it seemed a conjurer's trick. "What does it mean?" he cried in his disappointment. Then he returned to the spot where he had left the turtle, and saw the cord cut in a hundred pieces no longer than a finger's breadth. Then he perceived that the turtle had vanished like a magician, and anticipated danger for his own person. With troubled heart he made all speed out of the wood for home, casting anxious glances at the horizon.

Meanwhile the four friends, free of all injury, together, expressed their mutual affection, took new lease on life, and lived happily. And so

>If beasts enjoy so great a prize
>Of friendship, why should wonder rise
>In men, who are so very wise.

Loss of Gains

Here, then, begins Book IV, called "Loss of Gains." The first verse runs:

>Blind folly always has to pay
>For giving property away
>Because of blandishments and guile
>The monkey tricked the crocodile.

"How was that?" asked the princes. And Vishnusharman told the story of

The Monkey and the Crocodile

On the shore of the sea was a great rose-apple tree that was never without fruit. In it lived a monkey named Red-Face. Now one day a crocodile named Ugly-Mug crawled out of the ocean under the tree and burrowed in the soft sand. Then Red-Face said: "You are my guest, sir. Pray eat these rose-apples which I throw you. You will find them like nectar. You know the proverb:

>A fool or scholar let him be,
>Pleasant or hideous to see,
>A guest, when offerings are given,

> Is useful as a bridge to heaven.
> Ask not his home or education,
> His family or reputation,
> But offer thanks and sacrifice:
> For so prescribes the lawbook wise.

And again:

> By honoring the guests who come
> Wayworn from some far-distant home
> To share the sacrifice, you go
> The noblest way that mortals know.

And once again:

> If guests unhonored leave your door,
> And sadly sighing come no more,
> Your fathers and the gods above
> Turn from you and forget their love."

Thus he spoke and offered rose-apples. And the crocodile ate them and enjoyed a long and pleasant conversation with the monkey before returning to his home. So the monkey and the crocodile rested each day in the shade of the rose-apple tree. They spent the time in cheerful conversation on various subjects, and were happy.

Now the crocodile went home and gave his wife the rose-apples that he had not eaten. And one day she asked him: "My dear husband, where do you get such fruits? They are like nectar."

"My dear," he said, "I have an awfully good friend, a monkey named Red-Face. He gives me these fruits in the most courteous manner." Then she said: "If anyone eats such nectar fruit every day, his heart must be turned to nectar. So, if you value your wife, give me his heart, and I will eat it. Then I shall never grow old or sick, but will be a delightful companion for you."

But he objected: "In the first place, my dear, he is our adopted brother. Secondly, he gives us fruit. I cannot kill him. Please do not insist. Besides, there is a proverb:

> To give us birth, we need a mother;
> For second birth we need another:
> And friendship's brothers seem by far

More dear than natural brothers are."

But she said: "You have never refused me before. So I am sure it is a she-monkey. You love her and spend the whole day with her. That is why you will not give me what I want. And when you meet me at night, your sighs are hot as a flame of fire. And when you hold me and kiss me, you do not hug me tight. I know some other woman has stolen into your heart." Then the crocodile was quite dejected, and said to his wife:

> "When I am at your feet
> And at your service, sweet,
> Why do you look at me
> With peevish jealousy?"

But her face swam in tears when she heard him, and she said:

> "You love her, you deceiver;
> Your wishes never leave her;
> Her pretty shamming steals upon your heart.
> My rivalry is vain, sir;
> And so I pray abstain, sir,
> From service that is only tricky art.

"Besides, if you do not love her, why not kill her when I ask you? And if it is really a he-monkey, why should you love him? Enough! Unless I eat his heart, I shall starve myself to death in your house."

Now when he saw how determined she was, he was distracted with anxiety, and said: "Ah, the proverb is right:

> Remember that a single grab
> Suffices for a fish or crab,
> For fool or woman; and 'tis so
> For sot, cement, or indigo.

"Oh, what shall I do? How can I kill him?" With these thoughts in mind, he visited the monkey. Now the monkey had missed his friend, and when he saw him afflicted, he said:

"My friend, why have you not been here this long time? Why don't you speak cheerfully, and repeat something witty?" The crocodile replied: "My friend and brother, my wife scolded me today. She said: 'You ungrateful wretch! Do not show me your face. You are living daily at a friend's expense, and make him no return. You do not even show him the door of your house. You cannot possibly make amends for this. There is a saying:

> The Brahman-murderer or thief,
> Drunkard or liar, finds relief;
> While for ingratitude alone
> No expiation will atone.

" 'I regard this monkey as my brother-in-law. So bring him home, and we will make some return for his kindness. If you refuse, I will see you later in heaven.' Now I could not come to you until she had finished her scolding. And this long time passed while I was quarreling with her about you. So please come home with me. Your brother's wife has set up an awning. She has fixed her clothes and gems and rubies and all that, to pay you a fitting welcome. She has hung holiday garlands on the doorposts. And she is waiting impatiently."

"My friend and brother," said the monkey, your lady is very kind. It is quite according to the proverb:

> Six things are done by friends:
> To take, and give again;
> To listen, and to talk;
> To dine, to entertain.

"But we monkeys live in trees, and your home is in the water. How can I go there? Rather bring your lady here, brother, that I may bow down and receive her blessing."

The crocodile said: "My friend, our home is on a lovely sand-bank under the water. So climb on my back and travel comfortably with nothing to fear."

When the monkey heard this, he was delighted and said: "If that is possible, my friend, then hasten. Why delay? Here I am on your back."

But as he sat there and saw the crocodile swimming in the bottomless ocean, the monkey was terribly frightened and said: "Go slow, brother. My whole body is drenched by the great waves."

And the crocodile thought when he heard this: "If he fell from my back, he could not move an inch, the water is so deep. He is in my power. So I will tell him my purpose, and then he can pray to his most favorite god."

And he said: "Sir, I have deceived you and brought you to your death, because my wife bade me do it. So pray to your favorite god."

"Brother," said the monkey, "what harm have I done her or you? Why have you planned to kill me?"

"Well," replied the crocodile, "those nectar fruits tasted so sweet that she began to long to eat your heart. That is why I have done this."

Then the quick-witted monkey said: "If that is the case, sir, why didn't you tell me on shore? For then I might have brought with me another heart, very sweet indeed, which I keep in a hole in the rose-apple tree. As it is, I am forlorn in this heart, at being taken to her in vain, without my sweet heart."

When he heard this, the crocodile was delighted and said: "If you feel so, my friend, give me that other heart. And my cross wife will eat it and give up starving herself. Now I will take you back to the rose-apple tree." So he turned back and swam toward the rose-apple tree, while the monkey murmured a hundred prayers to every kind of a god. And when at last he came to shore, he hopped and jumped farther and farther, climbed up the rose-apple tree, and thought:

"Hurrah! My life is saved. Surely, the saying is a good one:

> We dare not trust a rogue; nor must
> We trust in those deserving trust:
> For danger follows, and we fall
> Destroyed and ruined, roots and all.

So today is my rebirthday."

The crocodile said: "My friend and brother, give me the heart, so that my wife may eat it and give up starving herself."

Then the monkey laughed, and scolded him, saying: "You fool! You traitor! How can anyone have two hearts? Go home, and never come back under the rose-apple tree. You know the proverb:

> Whoever trusts a faithless friend
> And twice in him believes,
> Lays hold on death as certainly
> As when a mule conceives."

Now the crocodile was embarrassed when he heard this, and he thought: "Oh, why was I such a fool as to tell him my plan? If I can possibly win his confidence again, I will do it." So he said: "My friend, she has no need of a heart. What I said was just a joke to test your sentiments. Please come to our house as a guest. Your brother's wife is most eager for you."

The monkey said: "Rascal! Go away this moment. I will not come. For

> The hungry man at nothing sticks;
> The poor man has his heartless tricks.
> Tell Handsome, Miss, that Theodore
> Will see him in the well no more."

"How was that?" asked the crocodile. And the monkey told the story of . . .

[**Note:** At this point another story is told. Again, this is an example of how tales link together. The following tale comes from Part 5 of the *Panchatantra*, *Ill-Considered Action*. This story does not have animal characters, but it follows the genre traits of the fable because the characters are typed and their actions picture a moral truth.]

The Four Treasure Seekers

In a certain town in the world were four Brahmans who lived as the best of friends. And being stricken with utter poverty, they took counsel together: "A curse, a curse on this business of being poor! For

> The well-served master hates him still;
> His loving kinsmen with a will
> Abandon him; woes multiply,
> While friends and even children fly;
> His high-born wife grows cool; the flash
> Of virtue dims; brave efforts crash—
> For him who has no ready cash.

And again:

> Charm, courage, eloquence, good looks,
> And thorough mastery of books
> (If money does not back the same)
> Are useless in the social game.

"Better be dead than penniless. As the story goes:

> A beggar to the graveyard hied
> And there 'Friend corpse, arise,' he cried;
> 'One moment lift my heavy weight
> Of poverty; for I of late
> Grow weary, and desire instead
> Your comfort: you are good and dead.'
> The corpse was silent. He was sure
> It was better to be dead than poor.

"So let us at any cost strive to make money. For the saying goes:

> Money gets you anything,
> Gets it in a flash:
> Therefore let the prudent get
> Cash, cash, cash.

"Now this cash comes to men in six ways. They are: (1) begging for charity, (2) flunkeyism at a court (3) farmwork, (4) the learned professions, (5) usury, (6) trade.

"However, among all these methods of making money, trade is the only one without a hitch in it.

> Kings' favor is a thing unstable;
> Crows peck at winnings charitable;
> You make, in learning the professions,
> Too many wearisome concessions
> To teachers; farms are too much labor;
> In usury you lend your neighbor
> The cash which is your life, and therefore
> You really live a poor man. Wherefore
> I see in trade the only living
> That can be truly pleasure-giving.
> Hurrah for trade!

"Now profitable trade has seven branches. They are: (1) false weights and balances, (2) price-boosting, (3) keeping a pawnshop, (4) getting regular customers, (5) a stock company, (6) articles deluxe such as perfumes, (7) foreign trade.

"Now the economists say:

> False weights and boosting prices to
> An overshameless sum
> And constant cheating of one's friends
> Are fit for social scum.

And again:

> Deposits in the house compel
> The pawnshop man to pray:
> If you will kill the owner, Lord,
> I'll give you what you say.

Likewise:

> The holder of a stock reflects
> With glee, though one of many:
> The wide world's wealth belongs to me;
> No other gets a penny.

Furthermore:

> Perfumery is first-class ware;
> Why deal in gold and such?
> Whatever the cost, you sell it for
> A thousand times as much.

"Foreign trade is the affair of the capitalist. As the book says:

> Wild elephants are caught by tame:
> So money-kings, devising
> A trap for money, capture it
> With far-flung advertising.

> The brisk commercial traveler,
> Who knows the selling game,
> Invests his money, and returns
> With twice or thrice the same.

And again:

> The crow, or good-for-naught, or deer,
> Afraid of foreign lands,
> In heedless slothfulness is sure
> To perish where he stands."

Having thus set their minds in order, and on foreign travel, they said farewell to home and friends, and started, all four of them. Well, there is wisdom in the saying:

> The man whose mind is money mad,
> From all his kinsmen flees;
> He hastens from his mother dear;
> He breaks his promises;
> He even goes to foreign lands
> Which he would not elect
> And leaves his native country. Well,
> What else do you expect?

So in time they came to the Avanti country, where they bathed in the waters of the Sipra, and adored great god Shiva. As they traveled farther, they met a master-magician named Terror-joy. And having greeted him in proper Brahman fashion, they all accompanied him to his monastery cell. There the magician asked them whence they came, whither they were going, and what was their object. And they replied: "We are pilgrims, seeking magic power. We have resolved to go where we shall find enough money, or death. For the proverb says:

> While water is given
> By fate out of heaven,
> If men dig a well,
> It bubbles from hell.
> Man's effort (sufficiently great)
> Can equal the wonders of fate.

And again:

> Success complete
> In any feat
> Is sure to bless
> True manliness.

> Man's effort (sufficiently great)
> Is just what a dullard calls fate.
>
> There is no toy
> Called easy joy,
> But man must strain
> To body's pain.
> Even Vishnu embraces his bride
> With arms that the churn-stick has tried.

"So disclose to us some method of getting money, whether crawling into a hole, or placating a witch, or living in a graveyard, or selling human flesh, or anything. You are said to have miraculous magic, while we have boundless daring. You know the saying:

> Only the great can aid the great
> To win their heart's desire:
> Apart from ocean, who could bear
> The fierce subaqueous fire?"

So the magician, perceiving their fitness as disciples, made four magic quills, and gave one to each, saying: Go to the northern slope of the Himalaya Mountains. And wherever a quill drops, there the owner will certainly find a treasure."

Now as they followed his directions, the leader's quill dropped. And on examining the spot, he found the soil all copper. So he said, "Look here! Take all the copper you want." But the others said, "Fool! What is the good of a thing which, even in quantity, does not put an end to poverty? Stand up. Let us go on." And he replied, "You may go. I will accompany you no farther." So he took his copper and was the first to turn back. The three others went farther. But they had traveled only a little way when the leader's quill dropped. And when he dug down, he found the soil all silver. At this he was delighted, and cried, "Look! Take all the silver you want. No need of going farther."

"Fool!" said the other two. "The soil was copper first, then silver. It will certainly be gold ahead. This stuff, even in quantity, does not relieve poverty so much."

"You two may go," said he. "I will not join you." So he took his silver and turned back.

The two went on until one quill dropped. When the owner dug down, he found the soil all gold. Seeing this, he was delighted, and said to his companion, "Look! Take all the gold you want. There is nothing beyond better than gold."

"Fool!" said the other. "Don't you see the point? First came copper, then silver, and then gold. Beyond there will certainly be gems. Stand up. Let us go farther. What is the good of this stuff? A quantity of it is a mere burden."

"You may go," he replied. "I will stay here and wait for you."

So the other went on alone. His limbs were scorched by the rays of the summer sun and his thoughts were confused by thirst as he wandered to and fro over the trails in the land of the fairies. At last, on a whirling platform, he saw a man with blood dripping down from his body, for a wheel was whirling on his head. Then he made haste and said, "Sir, why do you stand thus now with a wheel whirling on your head? In any case, tell me if there is water anywhere. I am mad with thirst."

The moment the Brahman said this, the wheel left the other's head and settled on his own. "My very dear sir," said he, "what is the meaning of this?"

"In the very same way," replied the other, "it settled on my head."

"But," said the Brahman, "when will it go away? It hurts terribly."

And the fellow said, "When someone who holds in his hand a magic quill such as you had, arrives and speaks as you did, then it will settle on his head."

"Well," said the Brahman, "how long were you here?" And the other asked:

"Who is king in the world at present?" On hearing the answer, "King Vinavatsa," he said, "When Rama was king, I was poverty stricken, procured a magic quill, and came here, just like you. And I saw another man with a wheel on his head and put a question to him. The moment I asked a question (just like you) the wheel left his head and settled on mine. But I cannot reckon the centuries. Then the wheel-bearer asked:

"My dear sir, how, pray, did you get food while standing thus?"

"My dear sir," said the fellow, "the god of wealth, lest his treasures be stolen, prepared this terror, that no magician might come so far. And if any should succeed in coming, he was to be freed from hunger and thirst, preserved from decrepitude and death, and was merely to endure this torture. So permit me to say farewell. You have set me free from a sizable misery. Now I am going home." And he went.

After he had gone, the gold-finder, wondering why his companion delayed, eagerly followed his prints. And having gone but a little way, he saw a man whose body was drenched with blood, tortured by a cruel wheel whirling on his head—and this man was his own companion. So he came and asked with tears, "My dear fellow, what is the meaning of this?"

"A whim of fate," said the other.

"But tell me," said he, "what has happened." And in answer to his question, the other told the entire history of the wheel. When the friend heard this, he scolded him, saying, "Well, I told you time and again not to do it. Yet from lack of sense you did not do as I said. Indeed, there is wisdom in the saying:

> Scholarship is less than sense;
> Therefore seek intelligence:
> Senseless scholars in their pride
> Made a lion; then they died."

"How was that?" asked the wheel-bearer. And the gold-finder told the story of . . .

Jataka Tales

Jataka tales are tales of Buddha's earlier births, often in animal form. The Buddha's incarnations occurred to help people learn the "dharma," Law, or Right Path, and so these ancient stories were rewritten to emphasize the Buddhist teachings. Some of these stories are Buddhist versions of tales that appear in the *Panchatantra* as the "Crocodile and the Monkey" in this collection. The oldest collection of Jataka tales is in Pali (an extinct language descended from Vedic, used in sacred texts of Buddhism) and includes 547 jatakas. The tales are believed to have appeared in written form in South Asia around 500 C.E. although their origins can be traced back to at least 300 B.C.E.

The Golden Deer

Once long ago, when Bramadatta was reigning in Benares, a rich merchant passed on his inheritance to his son, and then died. The young man lived foolishly. Quickly going through his father's fortune, he soon began borrowing and living on the credit of others. One day he awoke to find himself deep in debt, creditors knocking on his door. In desperation, he led them all to the bank of the Ganges River, claiming that he had a treasure buried there in the sandy bank. As they neared the riverbank he seemed to slip, and suddenly, losing his balance, tumbled in. The current bore him swiftly away. He called for help but not one of the creditors could brave that current, and standing helplessly on the shore they watched the youth as he was washed downstream, supposing he would be carried to his death. Now, all this had been part of that youth's hastily conceived plan. His creditors, he thought, seeing him washed downstream, would think him dead, and so he would be released, through this trick, from all liability. But the plan had a flaw. Swept away by the current the youth could not, in reality, regain the shore. His cries grew more and more desperate. He seemed lost, beyond all hope.

A magnificent Deer lay resting in a thicket. This Deer's fur was the color of gold. Its antlers gleamed like silver. Its hooves glistened as if lacquered. Its eyes shone like jewels. The Deer was, in fact, the Buddha in a former birth. Hearing the cries of that drowning man, the great Deer said to himself: "I hear the voice of a man. While I live I will not let him die! I will save his life for him!" Rising to his feet, the golden-furred Deer plunged through the thicket and leaped into the river. Forging through the swirling water he came to the drowning man, swam beneath him, lifted him up on his back, carried him safely to the shore, and brought him to the security of his own shelter.

For several days the Golden Deer nurtured the young man with wild fruits and nuts. Then, when he had fully recovered, the great Deer said, "In return for my kindness to you, when you return to the world of men, please tell no one of my hiding place. As I have saved you, now you must save me."

The young man, overflowing with gratitude, promised he would tell no one. Then, once again, the great Deer carried the young man on his back, bringing him now to the road. The Golden Deer returned to his hiding place in the forest, and the young man set off, back to the great and ancient city of Benares.

In the city of Benares, Queen Khema, wife to the great king Bramadatta, had a dream. She dreamed that a Deer whose fur shone like gold, whose antlers were like silver, whose hooves were bright as lacquer, and whose eyes shone like jewels appeared to her and taught her the ways of wisdom. She awoke filled with a longing to hear, in actuality, the wise teaching of this Golden Deer. Though it was only a dream, somehow she was sure that the Deer was real. She went to her husband and, relating the dream, begged that he offer a reward to anyone who might find this Golden Deer for her.

Bramadatta had tablets of gold put up on the walls of the city, offering a great chest of gold and jewels as well as an elephant from his own stable to carry the treasure to anyone who could lead his men to the golden-furred Deer. The young man, re-entering the city, read the tablets and was filled with longing for the treasure. Despite his promise, he went to the king and revealed what he knew. Then King Bramadatta, accompanied by a great company of men bearing spears and nets, had the young man guide them to the hiding place of the Golden Deer.

Surrounding the thicket, the men cried out loudly. The great Deer, hearing that cry, knew that he was trapped. "Where the king stands I shall be safe," he thought, and dashing from the thicket, he ran straight towards the king.

The king put an arrow to his bow and watched, thinking. "If the arrow frightens him well enough, he will stop. If he is for running, I will wound and weaken him that we may take him."

The Golden Deer ran like fire in the sunlight, straight toward the king, and stopped just before him. "Great King," he said, in a voice like golden honey, "I bear you no ill will. Nor will I run from you. But, tell me, who was it that led you to me?"

The king, enchanted by that wonderful voice, lowered his bow. Pointing to the young man, he said. "It was this one. He guided us here."

Then the great Deer recited this verse.

> "Upon the earth are many men of whom the proverb's true
> Better save a sinking log than one like you."

At this the king grew frightened and asked the meaning of the verse. "Of whom do you speak, great Deer?" he asked. "Are you talking of some bird or beast?"

"No, Great King," replied the Golden Deer. "I am speaking of a man. This young man here. He was drowning in the Ganges. I leaped in and saved him. I nursed him to health and, on my own back, carried him to the road when he was ready to travel. I asked only that he keep my whereabouts hidden. Now he has betrayed me."

When King Bramadatta heard of this, he drew his bowstring in wrath, ready to send an arrow through the traitor's heart. "Here is fit repayment for falsehood. Here is the treasure you deserve for such kindness to your benefactor," he proclaimed.

"No, Great King," said the Golden Deer. "Shame on this fool indeed, but no good men can approve of killing. Let him go and give him the treasure you promised. He has done what you have asked. Keep your word and I will serve you willingly."

"This Deer is goodness itself," the king thought. "It is worth much treasure, indeed, simply to have met him. That he will come willingly and share his wisdom is our good fortune."

"Go," said the king, to the young wastrel. "Take the reward I have promised and good riddance to all such uncharity."

Then the great Deer spoke again. "Great King, men say one thing with their lips yet often do another. Truly it is hard to trust the words of men."

"Great Deer," replied the king, "this day I offer you a boon. Do not think that all men are alike. I offer you the fulfillment of any wish you may choose. And I, for one, will keep my word to you, even should it mean I lose my kingdom or my life!"

"Then, Great King," replied the Golden Deer, "I choose that all creatures, from this day on, shall be free from danger. I ask that you give up all hunting."

The king granted this boon, and then led the great Deer back to the city of Benares. Having adorned the city with garlands and having garlanded the great Deer as well, he and the queen and all the people listened to the Great Being's discourse on truthfulness, charity, resoluteness, vigor, and other items of good character. Having strengthened the populace from king to beggar, each in his or her own determination to win mindfulness and attain wisdom, the Golden Deer left the city and returned to his forest where he resided as leader of a deer herd. King Bramadatta sent a proclamation through the land, and a drum beater marched through the city proclaiming, "Great Bramadatta extends protection to all creatures!" From that time on, all hunting ceased.

Now, after this, herds of deer ate the crops unhindered and all the people suffered. No one dared kill the deer or drive them away. An angry crowd gathered before the palace.

"Bramadatta in his greatness has ruined us," they complained. "Take back your proclamation, so that we may drive the deer from the fields. Do it or your kingdom is lost!"

But Bramadatta replied, "I have given my word and will not go back. Though I lose my kingdom or my life, to the Golden Deer I will remain true. The boon I have given him I will never deny."

The people departed in distress. Word of this spread through the land. The Great Being, the Golden Deer himself, heard of it and, gathering all the deer, gave them this order: "From this time forth, do not devour the fields of men. Bramadatta has, with his word, given us freedom. Let us, in return, repay him with restraint."

And so it was. Even to this day, the deer of that land do not feed in the cultivated fields. Men and animals share the land equally and the crops grow straight and tall in the golden sun.

The Monkey and the Crocodile

Once, there was a lazy and slow-witted crocodile, who liked nothing better than to lie in the sun on the warm, muddy banks of his lazy, green river. He would stretch out at the water's edge and, shutting his eyes tight, open his mouth wide in a great toothy grin. Then the little birds would fly in and out of his jaws, pecking at the scraps of food stuck between his yellowed teeth.

"Ah," he thought contentedly, digging his claws into the soft, gray mud, "but this is the life."

One day his wife crawled over to him and said, "Dear, have you noticed that monkey swinging around on the island lately?"

"Uh-huh," grunted the crocodile, keeping his eyes shut and his mouth open wide.

"Well," she went on, "he looks large and juicy. I bet his heart is very tender. Oh," she exclaimed at last, "how I wish I had that monkey's tender heart! Dear," she concluded, "wouldn't you go get his heart for me?"

"Uh-huh," sighed the crocodile. Closing his jaws with a *snap*!

He quietly opened his cold, yellow eyes and slowly crawled down the bank into the river. He moved his broad tail from side to side and slid through the cool, green water with hardly a ripple. But when he was only halfway across he slowly swung around and swam back to shore. His wife lay on the bank sunning herself. Her eyes were shut tight and her mouth was open wide.

"Dear," he said.

"Uh-huh?" she said. "Well," he said, "how am I going to catch that monkey when he's way up in the trees and I'm down here in the water?"

"Well," she answered, "you're big and strong, aren't you?" "Uh-huh," he exclaimed.

"Well, then, it's simple," she said. "Just offer to carry him across on your back to where all the sweet coconuts are ripening. Be a friend. You can do that, can't you?"

"Uh-huh," he said. And then, once again, the crocodile turned around and slid back into the water. Slowly he swam off, moving his broad tail steadily from side to side.

At this time the monkey was swinging around on the trees of his island. He was eating sweet fruits and enjoying himself in the warmth of the sun. "Ah," he reflected as he sat among the bright green leaves and the orange butterflies, "but life is good!"

Just at that moment the crocodile reached the shore of the monkey's island. Crawling along the sandy beach, he raised his knobbed and scaly head up toward the trees and called out in a very gentle-seeming voice indeed, "Brother monkey! Oh, Brother monkey!"

"Yes," answered the monkey, "what is it? Who is calling me?"

"It's me," answered the crocodile, "your friend from across the deep river, the crocodile. And I was just thinking, as the day is so warm and bright and the sun is shining so gloriously that I'd like to do something special for a friend today. My wife has told me that the mangos and coconuts on our side of the river are tender and juicy and ripe. And, as it's the perfect day for a swim, I'd be glad to take you for a ride over to where the sweetest ones are growing so you can eat to your heart's content. In fact," added the crocodile, with a great, toothy grin, "I'd be really glad to do it. Won't you come along?"

"Hmmm," said the monkey, scratching his head. "I don't know. Let me think it over. It is a nice day, and ripe coconuts and mangos would be nice." Then he asked, "Will you promise to go slow?"

"Slow?" grinned the crocodile, "Slow? Why, slow is my middle name! Just come along. You'll see."

"All right," said, the monkey, "I'll go with you." Then he hopped down out of the tree onto the crocodile's back, and off they went across the river.

As they swam along, the little waves washed and rippled over the crocodile's leathery hide, splashing among the rough scales and wetting the monkey's hands and feet. "Ooh, it's cold!" he cried.

"Cold?" leered the crocodile. "Cold?" You call that cold? Why, that's not cold—that's not cold yet at all!" And with that, he dived down through the green water to the gray, muddy bottom of the river.

The terrified monkey held on tight—*tight!*—and when they broke the surface again in a burst of mud and foam, the poor monkey gasped out from between his chattering teeth, "Friend crocodile, what are you doing? You nearly drowned me with your joke! Please be more careful. Have you forgotten your promise? Remember, my home is in the trees!"

"What joke?" said the crocodile with another nasty grin. "I'm taking you back to my wife. She wants your tender heart. And what she wants, she gets!"

"Oh!" said the monkey slowly, "I see. Yes, now I see! Well, friend," he added after a moment, "it's a good thing you told me. You almost made a terrible mistake."

"I did?" asked the crocodile, concerned. The smile left his jaws. "Please tell me. Friend monkey, how?"

"Why," said the monkey, "everyone knows I don't take something as important as my tender heart with me on ordinary little everyday trips. Oh, no, except for the most special occasions, I always leave my tender heart hanging safely at the top of the tallest tree on my island. A tender heart is a precious thing. Look back, friend crocodile. Don't you see it hanging there on that tall tree by the shore?"

The crocodile looked and, after a moment, thought that maybe he could see it. Yes, now he was sure of it! He did see it! He had almost made a terrible mistake.

"Listen, friend crocodile," said the monkey, "now that I know the whole story, why don't we just turn around? I'll go back and get my tender heart. It will be no trouble at all. In fact, I'd love to do it. Really! It will just take a minute. I bet your wife would have been upset," he added, as the crocodile turned slowly in the water and began to swim toward the island, "if you had brought me all the way over the water without my tender heart. That would have made for a really long delay. We would have had to come all the way back then, but now, you see, there's no real harm done."

"You're right," agreed the crocodile, "she never would have understood. You know," he added, "for a monkey you are a very good fellow."

"Thank you," said the monkey. "Glad I could help. Now, just wait here. I'll be back in a moment!" And with that the monkey took a tremendous leap straight up off the crocodile's back and bounded up into the branches of the tallest tree. Up, up, up he scampered, straight to the very top. Then, dancing on the highest branch he called out, "Foolish, foolish crocodile! Tender hearts don't grow on trees! A tender heart is the heart of compassion that feels kindly towards all things—

even silly crocodiles. One day you and your wife will surely have your own tender hearts. But until you do you won't find me riding on your back. Better head home now, my toothy friend. This joke's on you!"

And with that, the crocodile swam off, embarrassed and confused.

The wise monkey sat in the warmth of the golden sunshine drying his wet fur. Sweet fruits hung from the sturdy branches. Clear waves lapped against the shore below. "Ah!" he exclaimed, "how could that foolish crocodile have failed to find my tender heart?"

Aesopic Fables

The first collection of Aesopic fables in prose was made by Demetrius of Phalerum in the late fourth century B.C.E. It was primarily a handbook of narratives useful for orators and rhetoricians. Though it has not survived, it is believed to have been the source for Phaedrus (who wrote in Latin verse) and Babrius (who wrote in Greek verse), who provide us with the foundations for the Aesopic traditions.

Who was Aesop? Believed to be from Thrace, Aesop is identified as a sixth century B.C.E. slave on the island of Samos. His master freed him and he became known as a maker and teller of stories. Aristotle refers to an Aesopic fable in *Constitution of the Samians* and in his *Rhetoric* (II.20). However, it is highly unlikely that Aesop actually wrote anything or made public his fables. According to the literary standards of the time, prose lacked the artistic merit of epics, dramas, and lyric poetry. Aesopic fables, as prose works, would have had no respect as literature. What should be immediately notable about the Aesopic fable is that unlike the *Panchatantra*, *Jataka* tales, or many other fable traditions, the form is always brief and pithy. The narrative, with a few deft details, dependent on conventions about the particular animals, moves rapidly to make a political, social, or ethical point. There is no effort, as in many more elaborate fables to generate a novella in the form of a fable.

Babrius (ca. 70 C.E.), although probably a Roman citizen of Italian origins, wrote in Greek and lived in Syria. He claimed to be the first to have put Aesopic fables into verse. His collection comprises some 200 fables.

Phaedrus, a Roman citizen, was born ca. 18 B.C.E., on the Pierian Mountain, at the birthplace of the Muses, or so he claimed. He was educated in Roman schools, and dedicated himself to bringing the Greek literary traditions into Latin. His collection of Aesopic fables alludes to persecutions in the reign of Tiberius, but he lived to survive not only Tiberius and Sejanus, but also Caligula, and died sometime in the reign of Claudius or Nero (ca. 55 C.E.). His collection is the most important source for all the Aesopic fables that circulated in western Europe during the medieval and Renaissance periods.

The Vain Jackdaw

A jackdaw having dressed himself in feathers that had fallen from some peacocks, strutted about in the company of these birds, and tried to pass himself off as one of them. They soon found him out, and pulled their feathers from him so roughly, and in other ways so battered him, that when he would have rejoined his fellows, they in their turn, would have nothing to do with him, and drove him from their society.

The Fox and the Grapes

A hungry fox saw some fine bunches of grapes hanging from a vine that was trained along a high trellis, and did his best to reach them by jumping as high as he could into the air. But it was all in vain, for they were just out of reach: so he gave up trying, and walked away with an air of dignity and unconcern, remarking, "I thought those grapes were ripe, but I see now they are quite sour."

The Fox and the Crow

A Crow was sitting on a branch of a tree with a piece of cheese in her beak when a Fox observed her and set his wits to work to discover some way of getting the cheese. Coming and standing under the tree he looked up and said, "What a noble bird I see above me! Her beauty is without equal, the hue of her plumage exquisite. If only her voice is as sweet as her looks are fair, she ought without doubt to be Queen of the Birds." The Crow was hugely flattered by this, and just to show the Fox that she could sing she gave a loud caw. Down came the cheese, of course, and the Fox, snatching it up, said, "You have a voice, madam, I see: what you want is wits."

The Wolf and the Lamb

A Wolf came upon a Lamb straying from the flock, and felt some compunction about taking the life of so helpless a creature without some plausible excuse; so he cast about for a grievance and said at last, "Last year, sirrah, you grossly insulted me." "That is impossible, sir," bleated the Lamb, "for I wasn't born then." "Well," retorted the Wolf, "you feed in my pastures." "That cannot be," replied the Lamb, "for I have never yet tasted grass." "You drink from my spring, then," continued the Wolf. "Indeed, sir," said the poor Lamb, "I have never yet drunk anything but my mother's milk." "Well, anyhow," said the Wolf, "I'm not going without my dinner": and he sprang upon the Lamb and devoured it without more ado.

The Peacock and the Crane

A Peacock taunted a Crane about the dullness of her plumage. "Look at my brilliant colors," said she, "and see how much finer they are than your poor feathers." "I am not denying," replied the Crane, "that yours are far gayer than mine; but when it comes to flying I can soar into the clouds, whereas you are confined to the earth like any dunghill cock."

The Lion and the Mouse

A Lion tired with the chase, lay sleeping at full length under a shady tree. Some Mice scrambling over him while he slept, awoke him. Laying his paw upon one of them, he was about to crush him, but the Mouse implored his mercy in such moving terms that he let him go. Some time after, the Lion was caught in a net laid by some hunters, and, unable to free himself, made the forest resound with his roars. The Mouse whose life had been spared came, and with his little sharp teeth soon gnawed the ropes asunder, and set the Lion free.

The Oak and the Reeds

A violent storm uprooted an Oak that grew on the bank of a river. The Oak drifted across the stream and lodged among the Reeds. Wondering to find these still standing, he could not help asking them how it was that they had escaped the fury of the storm that had torn him up by the roots, "We bent our heads to the blast," said they, "and it passed over us. You stood stiff and stubborn till you could stand no longer."

The Frogs Asking for a King

Time was when the Frogs were discontented because they had no one to rule over them, so they sent a deputation to Jupiter to ask him to give them a king. Jupiter, despising the folly of their request, cast a log into the pool where they lived, and said that that should be their king. The Frogs were terrified at first by the splash, and scuttled away into the deepest part of the pool; but by and by, when they saw that the log remained motionless, one by one they ventured to the surface again, and before long, growing bolder, they began to feel such contempt for it that they even took to sitting upon it. Thinking that a king of that sort was an insult to their dignity, they sent to Jupiter a second time, and begged him to take away the sluggish King he had given them, and to give them another and better one. Jupiter, annoyed at being pestered in this way, sent a Stork to rule over them, who no sooner arrived among them than he began to catch and eat the Frogs as fast as he could.

The Hare and the Tortoise

A Hare was one day making fun of a Tortoise for being so slow on his feet. "Wait a bit," said the Tortoise. "I'll run a race with you, and I'll wager that I win." "Oh, well," replied the Hare, who was much amused at the idea, "let's try and see." And it was soon agreed that the Fox should set a course for them, and be the judge. When the time came both started off together, but the Hare was soon so far ahead that he laid down to rest. In the meantime, the Tortoise kept toddling along and reached his destination. When the Hare awoke, he hurried to the finishing line to find that the Tortoise had already arrived.

Town Mouse and Country Mouse

A Town Mouse and a Country Mouse were acquaintances, and the Country Mouse one day invited his friend to come and see him at his home in the fields. The Town Mouse came, and they sat down to a dinner of barleycorns and roots, the latter of which had a distinctly earthy flavor. The fare was not much to the taste of the guest, and presently he broke out with, "My poor dear friend, you live here no better than the ants. Now you should just see how I fare! My larder is a regular horn of plenty. You must come and stay with me, and I promise you, you shall live on the fat of the land." So when he returned to town he took the Country Mouse with him, and showed him into a larder containing flour and oatmeal and figs and honey and dates. The Country Mouse had never seen anything like it, and sat down to enjoy the luxuries his friend provided. But before they had well begun, the door of the larder opened and some one came in. The two Mice scampered off and hid themselves in a narrow and exceedingly uncomfortable hole. Presently, when all was quiet, they ventured out again; but some one else came in, and they scuttled again. This was too much for the visitor. "Good-bye," said he, "I'm off. You live in the lap of luxury, I can see, but you are surrounded by dangers; whereas at home I can enjoy my simple dinner of roots and corn in peace."

The Lion and the Bull

A Lion saw a fine fat Bull among a herd of cattle and cast about for some means of getting him in to his clutches; so he sent him word that he was sacrificing a sheep, and asked if he would do him the honor of dining with him. The Bull accepted the invitation, but, on arriving at the Lion's den, he saw a great array of saucepans and spits, but no sign of a sheep; so he turned on his heel and walked quietly away. The Lion called after him in an injured tone to ask the reason, and the Bull turned round and said, "I have reason enough. When I saw all your preparations it struck me at once that the victim was to be a Bull and not a sheep."

The net is spread in vain in sight of the bird.

Kalila and Dimna

Kalila and Dimna, called the most read book besides the Bible, has been translated into more than 40 languages. A translation of the *Panchatantra* into Pahlavi (literary Persian) around 570 C.E., it was later translated into Arabic by a Zoroastrian convert to Islam named Abdallah Ibn al-Moqaffa in 750 C.E. It made its way to Europe via this Arabic version which was made into Spanish in the 13th century as *Calila e Dimna*. It became one of the first books to be printed in German (1483). More commonly known as the *Fables of Bidpai* in Europe, La Fontaine used them in his collection of verse fables, produced in 17th century France. It was, along with the *Arabian Nights*, one of the most popular books in Europe in the 18th and 19th centuries.

The Monkey and the Tortoise

When the former story was finished, King Dabschelim commanded Bidpai to relate the history of the man, the success of whose pursuit in the fulfillment of his wishes is immediately followed by the loss of what he had obtained. The philosopher replied that the acquisition of a desired good is often attended with less difficulty than the means of preserving it, and whoever cannot secure the possession of what he has got into his power, may be compared to the tortoise in the following fable.

It is told of a certain king of the monkeys, whose name was Mahir, that being very old and infirm through age, was attacked by a young competitor for his crown, and was overcome and obliged to take flight; so he retired to the riverside, and discovered a fig-tree, and climbed up into it, and determined to make it his home. One day as he was eating of the fruit, a fig fell down, and the noise it occasioned by falling into the water delighted him so much that he never ate without repeating the experiment; and a tortoise, who was below, as often as a fig fell down, devoured it, and receiving during some days a regular supply, considered it as an attention towards him on the part of the monkey. Therefore he desired to become acquainted with the monkey, and in a short time they grew so intimate that they often conversed familiarly together. Now it happened that the tortoise stayed a long time away from his wife, who grew impatient at his absence, and complained of it to one of her neighbors, saying, "I fear something has happened unexpectedly to my husband." Her friend replied that if her husband was on the riverside, he would probably have made acquaintance with the monkey, and have been hospitably entertained by him.

Then after some days the tortoise returned to his home, and found his wife in a bad state of health, and apparently suffering very much, and he could not conceal the uneasiness that the sight of her occasioned. Expressing aloud his distress, he was interrupted by her friend, who said to him, "Your wife is very dangerously ill, and the physicians have prescribed for her the heart of a monkey." The tortoise replied, "This is no easy matter, for living as we do in the water, how can we possibly procure the heart of a monkey? However I will consult my friend about it." And he went to the shore of the river, and the monkey asked in terms of great affection what had detained him so long; and he answered, "The reluctance which I felt to repeat my visits, was owing to my being at a loss how to make you any suitable return for the kindness you have shown me; but I beg of you to add to the obligations under which you have laid me, by coming and passing some days with me; and as I live upon an island, which moreover abounds in fruit, I will take you upon my back, and swim over the water with you."

The monkey accepted the invitation and came down from the tree, and got upon the back of the tortoise, who, as he was swimming along with him, began to reflect on the crime that he harbored in his breast, and from shame and remorse hung down his head.

"What is the occasion," said the monkey, "of the sudden fit of sadness which is come upon you?"

"It occurs to me," answered the tortoise, "that my wife is very ill, and that I shall not therefore have it in my power to do the honors of my house in the manner I could wish."

"The intimations," replied the monkey, "which your friendly behavior has conveyed to me of your kind intentions, will supply the place of all unnecessary parade and ostentation."

Then the tortoise felt more at his ease, and continued his course. But on a sudden he stopped a second time, upon which the monkey, who was at a loss to account for this hesitation of the tortoise, began to suspect that something more was intended by it than he was able to discover; but repressing every thought that was injurious to the sincerity of his friend, he said to himself, "I cannot believe that his heart has changed, that his sentiments towards me have undergone an alteration. And that he intends to do me any mischief, however frequent such appearances may be in the world; and it is the voice of experience which directs the sensible man to look narrowly into the soul of those with whom he is connected by ties of affinity or friendship, by attending closely to everything that passes without them. For a wink of the eye, an expression which falls from the tongue, and even the motions of the body, are all evidences of what is going on in the heart; and wise men have laid it down as a rule, that when anyone doubts the sincerity of his friend, he should, by unremittingly observing every part of his conduct, guard against the possibility of being deceived by him. For if his suspicions are founded, he is repaid for the violence which they may have offered to his feelings, by the safety which they have procured him; and if they have been entertained without good grounds, he may at least congratulate himself on the measure of foresight which he possesses, which in no instance can be otherwise than serviceable to him." After having indulged himself in these reflections, he said to the tortoise, "Why do you stop a second time, and appear as if you were anxiously debating some question with yourself?"

"I am tormented," answered the tortoise, "by the idea, that you will find my house in disorder owing to the illness of my wife."

"Do not," said the monkey, "be uneasy on this account, for your anxiety will be of no use to you, but rather look out for some medicine, and food, which may be of service to your wife; for a person possessed of riches cannot employ them in a better manner, than either in works of charity during a time of want, or in the service of women."

"Your observation," answered the tortoise, "is just, but the physician has declared that nothing will cure her except the heart of a monkey."

Then the monkey reasoned with himself thus, "Fool that I am! Immoderate desires, which are not suited to my age, threaten me with destruction, and I now discover too late how true it is that the contented man passes his life in peace and security, whilst the covetous and ambitious live in trouble and difficulty; and I have occasion at this moment for all the resources of my understanding, to devise a means of escaping from the snare into which I have fallen."

Then he said to the tortoise, "Why did you not inform me of this sooner, and I would have brought my heart with me? It is the practice of the monkeys, when anyone goes out on a visit to a friend, to leave his heart at home, or in the custody of his family, so that he can look at his host's wife and still be without his heart."

"Where is your heart now?" said the tortoise.

"I have left it in the tree," answered the monkey, "and if you will return with me thither, I will bring it away."

The proposal was accepted, and the tortoise swam back with the monkey, who, as soon as he was near enough, sprung upon the shore, and immediately climbed up into the tree; and when the tortoise had waited for him some time, he grew impatient, and called out to him, to take his heart and come down, and not detain him any longer. "What," said the monkey, "do you think I am like the ass, of whom the jackal declared that he had neither heart nor ears?"

"How was this?" the tortoise asked.

[**Note:** Just as with the framed narratives in the books of the *Panchatantra*, this preceding narrative becomes the occasion for an exchange of stories between the monkey and the tortoise.]

Fables

BY MARIE DE FRANCE

Marie de France is a 12th century French writer famous for a collection of *Lais* or short verse stories treating of love, ladies, knights, and adventure. But she also produced the first vernacular collection of fables in Europe. These fables were very popular—23 manuscripts have survived—and they include both Aesopic material and her own narratives.

Prologue

Those persons, all, who are well-read,
Should study and pay careful heed
To fine accounts in worthy tomes,
To models and to axioms:
That which philosophers did find
And wrote about and kept in mind.
The sayings which they heard, they wrote,
So that the morals we would note;
Thus those who wish to mend their ways
Can think about what wisdom says.
The ancient fathers did just this.
The emperor, named Romulus,
Wrote to his son, enunciating,
And through examples demonstrating,
How it behooved him to take care
That no one trick him unaware.
Thus Aesop to his master wrote;
He knew his manner and his thought;
From Greek to Latin were transposed
Those fables found and those composed.
To many it was curious
That he'd apply his wisdom thus;

Yet there's no fable so inane
That folks cannot some knowledge gain
From lessons that come subsequent
To make each tale significant.
To me, who must these verses write,
It seemed improper to repeat
Some of the words that you'll find here.
Thus he commissioned me, however,
That one, the flower of chivalry,
Gentility and courtesy.
And when I'm asked by such a man,
I can do nothing other than
Labor with pained exactitude;
Though some may think that I am crude
In doing what he asked me for.
I'll start off with the first, therefore,
Of fables Aesop formulated
Which, for his master, he related.

The Wolf and the Lamb

This tells of wolf and lamb who drank
Together once along a bank.
The wolf right at the spring was staying
While lambkin down the stream was straying.
The wolf then spoke up nastily,
For argumentative was he,
Saying to lamb, with great disdain,
"You give me such a royal pain!"
The lamb made this reply to him,
"Pray sir, what's wrong?" "Are your eyes dim!
You've so stirred up the water here,
I cannot drink my fill, I fear.
I do believe I should be first,
Because I've come here dying of thirst."
The little lamb then said to him,
"But sir, 'twas you who drank upstream.
My water comes from you, you see."
"What!" snapped the wolf. "You dare curse me?"
"Sir, I had no intention to!"
The wolf replied, "I know what's true.
Your father treated me just so

Here at this spring some time ago—
It's now six months since we were here."
"So why blame me for that affair?
I wasn't even born, I guess."
"So what?" the wolf responded next;
"You really are perverse today—
You're not supposed to act this way."
The wolf then grabbed the lamb so small,
Chomped through his neck, extinguished all.
And this is what our great lords do,
The viscounts and the judges too,
With all the people whom they rule:
False charge they make from greed so cruel.
To cause confusion they consort
And often summon folk to court.
They strip them clean of flesh and skin,
As the wolf did to the lambkin.

The Crow and the Fox

It came to pass (and could be so)
That once in front of a window
Which in a pantry chanced to be,
A crow happened to fly by and see
That there, within, some cheeses lay
All spread out on a wicker tray.
He took a whole one; off he flew.
Along came fox, walked up to crow.
Fox very much desired the cheese;
He felt he had to eat a piece.
He thought he'd set a trap and see
If he could trick crow cunningly.
The fox cried out, "Oh God! Oh Sir!
Ah, what a noble bird is here!
I've never seen in all this world
A sight as lovely as this bird!
Would that his songs were just as fair,
Beyond pure gold he would compare!"
All this grand praise the crow could hear:
How through the world he had no peer.
His voice he thought in song he'd raise;
His singing never lost him praise.

And so crow sang, his mouth agape;
And thus he let the cheese escape.
No sooner did it hit the ground,
Than fox, he seized it in a bound.
He had no interest in the song;
The cheese he'd wanted all along.
A lesson's here about the proud
Who wish with fame to be endowed:
If you should flatter them and lie,
You'll find they readily comply.
They'll spend their all quite foolishly
When they receive false flattery.

The Lion and the Mouse

It's said a lion was asleep
Where he lived in a forest deep.
Some little mice 'round where he lay
Came to amuse themselves and play.
One of them ran—not taking care—
Over the lion and woke him there.
The lion now was furious.
He grabbed the mouse; so wroth he was,
He wished to bring the mouse to court.
She pleaded that she'd surely not
Acted at all deliberately.
And soon the lion set her free.
There's little honor anyhow,
He said, if he should kill her now.
Then just a short time after that,
A man, it is reported, had
Prepared a deep, wide-open pit.
That night the lion fell into it.
Within the pit, quite terrified
That he'd be killed, he roared and cried.
Hearing this, mouse came hastily,
Though she knew not who it might be.
Then when she saw by trap o'ertaken
The one whom in the woods she'd wakened,
She asked him what it was he sought.
He answered her that he was caught
And grieved he might be killed in there.

The mouse responded, "Have no fear!
I'll now return to you the guerdon
That you once gave me by your pardon
When over you my feet did bound.
Now with your paw scratch at the ground
Until your foothold is quite stable.
Then you should climb as best you're able
Till up out of the pit you'll be.
And I'll arrange to bring with me
More mice who will their help provide
To cut the ropes with which you're tied,
And nets as well, about you strained;
You'll thus no longer be contained."
Then this advice which the mouse gave him
The lion followed, and it saved him.
Thus he escaped out of the pit:
Humility brought benefit.
And so this model serves to show
A lesson wealthy men should know
Who over poor folks have much power.
If these should wrong them, unaware,
The rich should show them charity,
For unto them the same might be:
The rich may need the poor man who
Can better tell him what to do
When he's by sudden need hard pressed,
Than can his friends, even the best.

The Crow in Peacock's Feathers

In olden times there was a crow
Who chanced along a road to go
And peacock plumes and feathers found.
Studying himself, up and down,
He thought he was the worst bird e'er
For he had never looked so fair.

He plucked out all his plumes; when done,
He had not left a single one.
He did in peacock feathers dress
To make his body beauteous,
And went to join the peacock flock.

To them, he seemed like no peacock
And was, by their wings, buffeted.
What worse things they could do, they did!
He wished to be a crow again—
As he had been—and look like one.
But no one recognized him, so
They beat him up; they killed the crow.
And this with many folks, you'll see:
They've honor and prosperity,
And yet they want to get much more
Than their capacity to store.
They gain naught from their greediness
And lose their goods to foolishness.

The Beetle

A beetle's story I'll relate
That I found written down of late.
This beetle lay in a dunghill.
One day, when he had had his fill,
He went outside; his dunghill eyeing,
He saw, above, an eagle flying.
So proud this eagle seemed to be,
His heart was filled with jealousy.
To other beetles he observed,
They'd by their Maker been disserved:
She'd made the eagle courtly, grand,
But they were neither bird nor man.
When full, the beetles can't take wing;
Hungry, they can't be journeying.
"This whole day long, I fixed my gaze
On eagle, whom we deem our liege.
He flew so high up, out of view,
And came down when he wanted to.
His voice, of soft and easy tone,
Is yet no louder than my own.
My body glistening is, likewise,
As much as his, despite his size.
One thing is absolutely clear:
No matter what the time of year
I won't stay in a dung heap more!
With other birds I'd rather soar—

And I will live just as they do
And go wherever they go, too!"
With these words he began to sing
And make a dreadful clamoring.
After eagle, the beetle hopped;
To fly the higher was his thought.
Before the beetle far had gone,
He found himself bewildered, stunned,
And neither could fly higher still
Nor yet go back to his dunghill.
And he was famished, wanted food,
Sorely complained, loud as he could,
And did not care if any heard
Nor if they mocked him, any bird.
(No more than fox did long ago
When other beasts thought him so low.)
"I don't care whether I am thought
A worm or bird—or even that
I come in horse's excrement.
I'm sad and sick from famishment!"
And thus with prideful folk we see
That their own judges they will be:
What they can't do, they undertake,
And then find out they must turn back.

Epilogue

To end these tales I've here narrated
And into Romance tongue translated,
I'll give my name, for memory:
I am from France, my name's Marie.
And it may hap that many a clerk
Will claim as his what is my work.
But such pronouncements I want not!
It's folly to become forgot!
Out of my love for Count William,
The doughtiest in any realm,
This volume was by me created,
From English to Romance translated.
This book's called Aesop for this reason:
He translated and had it written
In Latin from the Greek, to wit.

King Alfred, who was fond of it,
Translated it to English hence,
And I have rhymed it now in French
As well as I was competent.
I pray to God omnipotent
To let me to such work attend
And thus to Him my soul commend.

The Book of Good Love

BY JUAN RUIZ

These fables come from *The Book of Good Love*, a long narrative poem written in Castilian Spanish by Juan Ruiz (ca. 1340). The work is a fictional autobiography that includes a huge range of medieval literary genres: fables, fabliaux, allegories, and parodies as well as the numerous mostly unsuccessful attempts of the first person narrator to seduce many women, a number of digressions on interpretive theory, and sincere devotional poetry addressed to the Virgin Mary.

The Fable of the Dog That Was Carrying a Piece of Meat in His Mouth

A greedy hound was wading in a river, as I deem,
And holding fast a piece of meat between his drooling jaws,
Reflected in the water was a second dog, it seemed.
He tried to grab the meat from it and dropped his in the stream.

Deceived by his reflection and his very vain impression,
The mastiff lost the chunk of meat that he already carried.
He didn't get what he desired, his wish was wrong and stupid.
He thought to gain, but lost what once had been in his possession.

This happens every day to a man as covetous as that.
He hopes to gain by you, but loses wealth and never wins.

Out of these evil roots is born all evil that has been.
This wicked covetousness for all mankind is mortal sin!

When any man keeps safe, secure and fast in his domain
A stock of all the best, most precious things he can attain,

He never ought to risk them for a whim that may be vain.
For he who loses what he has, an empty profit gains.

The Fable of the Lion
Who Killed Himself in Anger

Vainglorious, full of wrath, a lion, whose pride was infinite,
And who was cruel and harmful, bane to all the animals,
Once killed himself, in mighty anger and a raging fit.
I'll tell the fable to you—may you profit much by it.

The proud and haughty lion, when he was a youthful beast,
Was used to hunt his prey with wrath and courage unappeased,
And some he killed outright, on others he inflicted wounds.
But weakness and old age came on him and his strength decreased.

This news the animal messengers to every tribe relayed.
They all were glad of it—now they could roam alone in peace
And marched against him to avenge the marks his teeth had made.
Even the stupid donkey marched in front of this parade.

They gave the lion a spate of wounds—to all he had to yield.
The wild boar, full of burning anger, gored him with his tusks.
The big bull and the steer impaled him on their brutal horns.
The lazy donkey with a stroke left him well marked and sealed:

He struck two mighty kicks, aimed at the forehead of his lord.
The haughty lion in anger dug into his heart his claws
And died by his own nails—not by the others' blows at all.
Vainglory and wrath, indeed, gave him a very poor reward.

The man who has position, honor and authority,
Should not do unto others what he'd not want done to him.
For he can flatly lose his power and that quite suddenly,
And what he's done to others, he can get in kind from them.

Mathnawi

BY JALAL-UD-DIN RUMI

Jalal-ud-Din Rumi was born in 1207 and died in 1273. He is the most eminent medieval Sufi, or Islamic mystic, poet. Written in Persian, his *Mathnawi* comprises six books with 26,000 verses and it took 15 years to complete. The subject of the *Mathnawi*, like the Indian *niti-shastras* (see *Panchatantra*) focuses on conduct in life as well as speculations about the meaning of life. The *Mathnawi* includes many fables, of which the following parable-fable is an example.

The Unseen Elephant

The Elephant was in a dark house: some Hindus had brought it for exhibition.

As seeing it with the eye was impossible, everyone felt it in the dark with the palm of his hand.

The hand of one fell on its trunk: he said, "This creature is like a water-pipe."

Another touched its ear: to him it appeared like a fan.

Another handled its leg: he said, "I found the Elephant's shape to be like a pillar."

Another laid his hand on its back: he said, "Truly this Elephant resembles a throne."

Had there been a candle in each one's hand, the difference would have gone out of their words.

Fables

BY LEONARDO DA VINCI

Leonardo da Vinci (1452-1519), an Italian writer, painter, and inventor, who is famous for his paintings of the Mona Lisa and the Last Supper, was equally brilliant in almost every task he undertook. He was also an inventor (bicycle, airplane, etc.), a writer, and the versatile intellectual that typifies the "Renaissance man." In addition to all his varied activities, he found time to write a series of fables, from which the following are selected.

The Spider in the Keyhole

A spider, after exploring the whole house, inside and out, decided to hide in the keyhole.

What an ideal refuge, he thought. Who would ever guess he was there? And the spider could peep over the edge of the hole and look all round.

"Up there," he said to himself, glancing up at the stone lintel, "I shall spread a net for the flies. Down here," he added, looking at the step, "I shall spread another for the grubs. Here, by the side of the door, I shall set a little trap for the mosquitoes."

The spider was overjoyed. Being in the keyhole gave him a new and wonderful feeling of security. It was so narrow, dark, and lined with iron. It seemed more impregnable than a fortress, and safer than any armor.

While he was indulging in these delightful thoughts, the spider heard the sound of approaching footsteps. He crept back into the depths of his refuge.

But the spider had forgotten that the keyhole was not made for him. Its rightful possession, the key, thrust into the lock and pushed him out.

The Flea and the Sheep

A flea, who lived in the smooth hair of a dog, one day noticed the pleasant smell of wool.

"What is going on?"

He gave a little jump and saw that his dog had gone to sleep leaning against the fleece of a sheep.

"That fleece is exactly what I need," said the flea. "It is thicker and softer, and above all safer. There is no risk of meeting the dog's claws and teeth which go in search of me every now and then. And the sheep's wool will certainly feel more pleasant."

So without thinking too much about it, the flea moved house, leaping from the dog's coat to the sheep's fleece. But the wool was thick, so thick and dense that it was not easy to penetrate to the skin.

He tried and tried, patiently separating one strand from another, and laboriously making a way through. At last he reached the roots of the hair. But they were so close together that they practically touched. The flea had not even a tiny hole through which to attack the skin.

Tired, bathed in sweat and bitterly disappointed, the flea resigned himself to going back to the dog. But the dog had gone away.

Poor flea! He wept for days and days with regret for his mistake.

The Falcon and the Duck

Every time he went duck hunting, the noble falcon was furious. Those ducks almost always succeeded in making a fool of him, diving under water at the very last moment, and remaining submerged longer than he could hover in the air waiting for them.

One morning, the falcon decided to try again. After circling for some time with outspread wings to review the situation, and carefully picking out the duck to be captured, the noble bird of prey dropped like a stone. But the duck was quicker, and dived headfirst.

"This time I'm coming after you," cried the falcon in fury, and dived as well.

The duck, seeing the falcon under the water, gave a flick of his tall, came to the surface, opened his wings and began to fly. The falcon's feathers were soaked, and he could not fly.

The ducks flew above him, saying, "Goodbye, falcon! I can fly in your sky, but in my water you sink!"

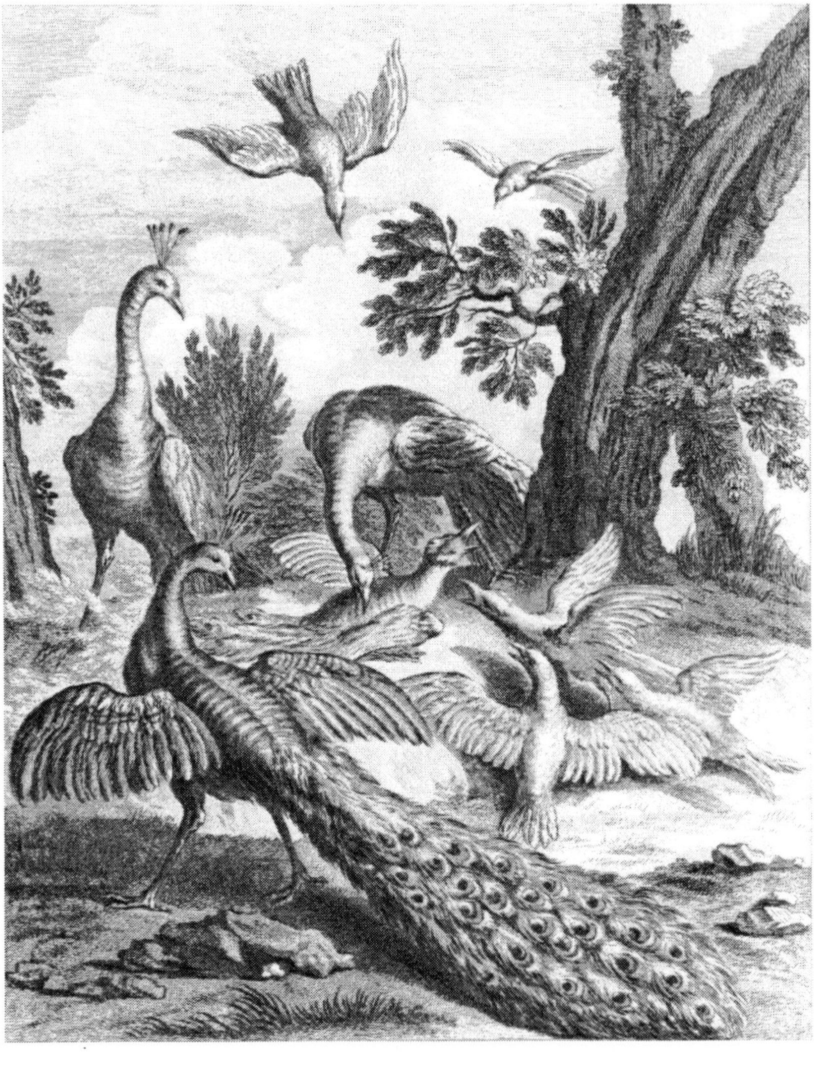

Fables

BY JEAN DE LA FONTAINE

Jean de la Fontaine (1621–1695) is the quintessential fabulist. The son of an important royal functionary, whose title of "Master of Streams and Forests" bespeaks the closeness to woodland life and creatures that is a hallmark of his fables, La Fontaine grew up in and around the forested areas of Chateau-Thierry, 60 miles northeast of Paris. Having succeeded to his father's position upon the latter's death, La Fontaine nonetheless squandered his fortune, moved to Paris, and began writing poetry. In addition to his fables, he wrote short tales, lyric poetry, a comedy, and a novel. Invariably out of favor with the king, he was admitted to the Académie Française in 1684 after several unsuccessful petitions.

Like many fabulists, La Fontaine began as a translator of the Aesopic tradition, publishing a first collection in 1668, *Selected Fables Put to Verse*, that included a "Life of Aesop" and a preface where the French poet elaborated his concept of the fable, which he views as "composed of two parts, of which one can be called the Body, the other the Soul. The Body is the Fable; the Soul, is the Moral." In terms of content, what La Fontaine makes most explicit is the function of the beast in fables as social and political allegory of human mores: "The properties of animals and their various characteristics are expressed [in these fables]; and consequently, ours also, since we are the sum of all that is good and all that is bad in creatures without reason. . . . Hence, these fables are a painting in which we all find ourselves depicted." Indeed, the typical La Fontaine fable conjoins a close observational familiarity with animals' behavior in their wild settings with an implicit indictment of the cynical power politics that defined life at the French court of Louis XIV. The refractory gist of his fables was not lost on contemporary readers. During the French Revolution, his portrait appeared alongside those of Voltaire and Rousseau as one of the event's intellectual forebears.

It is not surprising, then, that La Fontaine quickly developed as a writer of fables, increasingly inflecting his "verse translations" with his distinctive imprint. As his production grew, he began to write his own fables as well as casting a much wider net in terms of his sources of inspiration. Most notably, he made particular use of the Bidpai (see *Kalila and Dimna*) in his later work, as well as drawing inspiration from his own powers of observation to contest René Descartes's claim that only human beings are intelligent and willful creatures while animals are simply machines subject to physical laws. At the same time, La Fontaine himself modernized the fable tradition by referring to contemporary events and inventions, such as the telescope.

La Fontaine's legacy was, ironically, to become one of the cornerstones of the French educational system in the 19th century. Especially under the Third Republic, the fables became a prime vehicle for the inculcation of bourgeois values and socialization of children—a far cry from their 17th-century inspiration in Niccolò Machiavelli's perception of a social world governed not by moral principle but by power and self-interest.

The Grasshopper and the Ant

The Grasshopper so blithe and gay,
Sang the summer time away.
Pinched and poor the spendthrift grew,
When the sour north-easter blew.
In her larder not a scrap,
Bread to taste, nor drink to lap.
To the Ant, her neighbor she
Went to moan her penury,
Praying for a loan of wheat,
Just to make a loaf to eat,
Till the sunshine came again.
"All I say is fair and plain,
I will pay you every grain,
Principal and interest too,
Before harvest, I tell you,
On my honor, every pound,
Ere a single sheaf is bound."
The Ant's a very prudent friend,

Never much disposed to lend;
Virtues great and failings small,
This her failing least of all.
Quoth she, "how spent you the summer?"
"Night and day, to each new comer
I sang gaily, by your leave;
Singing, singing, morn and eve."
"You sang? I see it at a glance.
Well, then, now's the time to dance."

The Raven and the Fox

Master Raven, perched upon a tree,
Held in his beak a savory piece of cheese;
Its pleasant odor, borne upon the breeze,
Allured Sir Reynard, with his flattery.
"Ha! Master Raven, 'morrow to you, sir;
How black and glossy! Now, upon my word,
I never—beautiful! I do aver.
If but your voice becomes your coat, no bird
More fit to be the Phoenix of our wood—
I hope, sir, I am understood?"
The Raven, flattered by the praise,
Opened his spacious beak, to show his ways
Of singing: down the good cheese fell.
Quick the fox snapped it. "My dear sir, 'tis well,"
He said. "Know that a flatterer lives
On him to whom his praise he gives;
And my dear neighbor, an' you please,
This lesson's worth a slice of cheese."
The Raven, vexed at his consenting,
Flew off, too late in his repenting.

The Wolf and the Lamb

The reasoning of the strongest carries the most weight,
None can gainsay it, or dare prate,
No more than one would question Fate.
A Lamb his thirst was very calmly slaking,
At the pure current of a woodland rill;
A grisly Wolf, by hunger urged, came making
A tour in search of living things to kill.
"How dare you spill my drink"?" he fiercely cried.

There was grim fury in his very tone:
"I'll teach you to let beasts like me alone."
"Let not your Majesty feel wrath," replied
The Lamb, "nor be unjust to me, from passion;
I cannot, Sir, disturb in any fashion
The stream which now your Royal Highness faces,
I'm lower down by at least twenty paces."
"You spoil it!" roared the Wolf; "and more, I know,
You slandered me but half a year ago."
"How could I do so, when I scarce was born?"
The Lamb replied; "I was a suckling then."
"Then 'twas your brother held me up to scorn."
"I have no brother." "Well, 'tis all the same;
At least 'twas some poor fool that bears your name.
You and your dogs, both great and small
Your sheep and shepherds, one and all,
Slander me, if men say but true,
And I'll revenge myself on you."
Thus saying, he bore off the Lamb
Deep in the wood, far from its dam.
And there, not waiting judge or jury,
Fell to, and ate him in his fury.

Death and the Woodcutter

Poor Woodcutter, covered with his load
Bent down with boughs and with a weary age,
Groaning and stooping, made his sorrowing stage
To reach his smoky cabin; on the road,
Worn out with toil and pain, he seeks relief
By resting for awhile, to brood on grief.
What pleasure has he had since he was born?
In this round world was there one more forlorn?
Sometimes no bread, and never, never rest.
Creditors, soldiers, taxes, children, wife.
The corvée. Such a life!
The picture of a miserable man—look east or west.
He calls on Death—for Death calls everywhere—
Well—Death is there.
He comes without delay,
And asks the groaner if he needs his aid.
"Yes," said the Woodman, "help me in my trade.

Put up these faggots—then you need not stay."

Death is a cure for all, say I,
But do not budge from where you are;
BETTER TO SUFFER THAN TO DIE,
Is man's old motto, near and far.

The Oak and the Reed

The Oak said one day to a river Reed,
"You have a right with Nature to fall out.
Even a wren for you's a weight indeed;
The slightest breeze that wanders round about
Makes you first bow, then bend;
While my proud forehead, like an Alp, braves all,
Whether the sunshine or the tempest fall—
A gale to you to me a zephyr is.
Come near my shelter: you'll escape from this;
You'll suffer less, and everything will mend.
I'll keep you warm
From every storm
And yet you foolish creatures needs must go,
And on the frontiers of old Boréas grow.
Nature to you has been, I think, unjust."
"Your sympathy," replied the Reed, "is kind,
And to my mind
Your heart is good; and yet dismiss your thought.
For us, no more than you, the winds are fraught
With danger, for I bend, but do not break.
As yet, a stout resistance you can make,
And never stoop your back, my friend;
But wait a bit, and let us see the end."
Black, furious, raging, swelling as he spoke,
The fiercest wind that ever yet had broke
From the North's caverns bellowed through the sky.
The Oak held firm, the Reed bent quietly down.
The wind blew faster, and more furiously,
Then rooted up the tree that with its head
Had touched the high clouds in its majesty,
And stretched far downwards to the realms of dead.

The Frogs Who Asked for a King

Of Democrats the Frogs grew tired,
And unto Monarchy aspired;
Clamor so loud, that from a cloud
Great Jove in pity dropped a King,
Silent and peaceful, all allowed
And yet he fell with such a splash, the thing,
Quite terrified those poor marsh folks,
   Not fond of jokes,
Foolish and timid, all from him hid;
  And each one brushes
To hide in reeds, or sneak in rushes;
And from their swampy holes, poor little souls!
For a long time they dared not peep
At the great giant, still asleep.
   And yet the monarch of the bog,
   Was but A LOG,
Whose solemn gravity inspired with awe
The first who venturing saw:
He hobbled somewhat near,
With trembling and with fear;
Then others followed, and another yet,
Until a crowd there met.
At last the daring mob grew bolder,
And leaped upon the royal shoulder.
Good man, he did not take it ill,
But as before kept still.
Soon Jupiter is deafened with the din—
"Give us a king who'll move," they all begin.
The monarch of the gods sends down a Crane,
Who with a vengeance comes to reign.
He gobbles and he munches,
He sups and lunches
Till louder still the Frogs complain.
"Why, see!" great Jupiter replied,
"How, foolishly you did decide.
You'd better kept your first—the last is worst.
You must allow, if you are fair,
King Log was calm and debonair:
With him, then, be ye now content,
For fear a third, and worse, be sent."

The Animals Sick of the Plague

A malady that Heaven sent
On earth, for our sin's punishment—
The Plague (if I must call it right),
Fit to fill Hades in a night—
Upon the animals made war;
Not all die, but all stricken are.
They scarcely care to seek for food,
For they are dying, and their brood.
The Wolves and Foxes crouching keep,
Nor care to watch for timorous Sheep.
Even the very Turtle-doves
Forget their little harmless loves.
The Lion, calling counsel, spoke—
"Dear friends, upon our luckless crown
Heaven misfortune has sent down,
For some great sin. Let, then, the worst
Of all our race be taken first,
And sacrificed to Heaven's ire;
So healing Mercury, through the fire,
May come and free us from this curse,
That's daily growing worse and worse.
History tells us, in such cases
For patriotism there a place is.
No self-deception—plain and flat
Search each his conscience, mind you that.
I've eaten several sheep, I own.
What harm had they done me?—why none.
Sometimes—to be quite fair and true—
I've eaten up the shepherd too.
I will devote myself; but, first,
Let's hear if any has done worst.
Each must accuse himself, as I
Have done; for justice would let die
The guiltiest one. The Fox replied,
You are too good to thus decide.
Your Majesty's kind scruples show
Too much of delicacy. No!
What! eating sheep—the paltry—base,
Is that a sin? You did the race,
In munching them, an honor—yes,

I'm free, your highness, to confess.
And as for shepherds, they earn all
The evils that upon them fall:
Being of those who claim a sway
(Fantastic claim!) o'er us, they say."
Thus spoke the Fox the flatterer's text.
The Tiger and the Bear came next,
With claims that no one thought perplexed.
In fact, more quarrelsome they were,
The fewer grew the cavillers there.
Even the humblest proved a saint:
None made a slanderous complaint.
The Ass came in his turn, and said,
"For one thing—I myself upbraid.
Once, in a rank green abbey field,
Sharp hunger made me basely yield.
The opportunity was there;
The grass was rich; the day was fair.
Some demon tempted me: I fell,
And cleared my bare tongue's length, pell-mell."
Scarce had he spoken ere they rose
In arms, nor waited for the close.
A Wolf, half lawyer, made a speech,
And proved this creature wrong'd them each
And all, and they must sacrifice
This scurvy wretch, who to his eyes
Was steep'd in every wickedness.
Doom'd to the rope, without redress,
"Hang him at once! What! Go and eat
An Abbot's grass, however sweet!
Abominable crime!" they cry;
"Death only clears the infamy."
If you are powerful, wrong or right,
The court will change your black to white.

The Power of Fables

To M. de Barillon.

How can a great ambassador descend
To simple tales a patient ear to lend
How could I trifling verses to you bring

Or dare with transient playfulness to sing?
For if, sometimes, I vainly tried to soar,
Would you not only deem me rash once more?
You have more weighty matters to debate
Than of a Weasel and a Rabbit's fate.
Read me, or read me not; but, oh, debar
All Europe banding against us in war.
Lest from a thousand places there arise
Fresh enemies our legions to surprise.
England already wearies of her rest,
And views our king's alliance as a jest.
Is it not time that Louis sought repose?
What Hercules but wearies of his blows
At the huge Hydra?—will it show its might,
And press again the lately ended fight,
By thrusting forth another head to meet,
At his strong sinewy arm, a fresh defeat?
If your mind, pliant, eloquent, and strong,
Could soften hearts, and but avert this wrong,
I'd sacrifice a hundred sheep to you—
A pretty thing for a poor bard to do.
Have then, at least, the kindness graciously
This pinch of incense to receive from me.
Accept my ardent vows, and what I write:
The subject suits you that I here indite.
I'll not repeat the praises Envy owns
Are due to you, who need not fear her groans.
In Athens' city, fickle, vain, of old,
An Orator, who dangers manifold
Saw crowding in his country, one day went
Up in the tribune, with the wise intent
With his skill'd tongue, and his despotic art
Towards a republic to force every heart.
He spoke with fervor 'bout the common weal;
They would not listen: they were hard as steel.
The Orator, to rouse them, had recourse
To metaphors of greater fire and force,
To sting the basest. He awoke the dead.
He, Zeus-like, flamed and thunder'd o'er each head:
The wind bore all away,—yes, every word
The many-headed monster had not heard:
They ran to see the rabble children play,

Or two boys fighting made them turn away.
What did the speaker do?—he tried once more:
"Ceres," he said, "once made, we hear, a tour.
An Eel and Swallow follow'd her;
A river gave them some demur.
The Eel it swam: the Swallow flew,
Now what I tell you's really true."
And as he utter'd this, the crowd
"And Ceres, what did she?" cried loud.
"Just what she did;"—then pious rage
Stirr'd him to execrate the age.
"What children's tales absorb your mind,
Careless of all the woes behind!
Thou only careless Grecian state,
What Philip does you should debate."
At this reproach the mob grew still,
And listen'd with a better will
Such silence a mere fable won!
We're like the Greeks all said and done.
And I myself, who preach so well,
If any one to me would tell
"La Peau d'Ane," I should, with delight,
Listen for half the livelong night.
The world is old, as I have I heard,
And I believe it, on my word;
Yet still, though old, I'm reconciled
To entertain it like a child.

The Rat and the Elephant

In France there's many a man of small degree
Fond of asserting his own mightiness
A "nobody" turns "somebody." We see
In this the nation's natural flightiness.
In Spain men are not vain; their high-flown schools
Have made them proud, yet have not made them fools.
A tiny Rat saw a huge Elephant
Travelling slowly with his equipage;'
'Mongst beasts a sultan, knowing not a want.
His suite comprised within a monstrous cage
His household gods, his favorite dog and cat,
His parroquet, his monkey, and all that.

The Rat, astonished to see people stare
At SO much bulk and state, which took up all
The space where he of right should have his share,
Upon the citizens began to call:
"Fools know you not that smallest rats are equal
To biggest elephants?" (Alas the sequel.)
"Is it his monstrous bulk you're staring at?
It can but frighten little girls and boys;
Why, I can do the same. You see, a Rat
Is scarce less than an Elephant." A noise!
The Cat sprang from her cage and, with one pant,
The Rat found he was not an Elephant.

The Hare and the Frogs

One day sat dreaming in his form a Hare,
(And what but dream could one do there?)
With melancholy much perplexed
(With grief this creature's often vexed).
People with nerves are to be pitied,
And often with their dumps are twitted;
Can't even eat, or take their pleasure;
"Ennui," he said, "torments their leisure.
See how I live: afraid to sleep,
My eyes all night I open keep.
'Alter your habits,' someone says;
But Fear can never change its ways:
In honest faith shrewd folks can spy,
That men have fear as well as I."
Thus the Hare reasoned; so he kept
Watch day and night, and hardly slept;
Doubtful he was, uneasy ever;
A breath, a shadow, brought a fever.
It was a melancholy creature,
The veriest coward in all nature;
A rustling leaf alarmed his soul,
He fled towards his secret hole.
Passing a pond, the Frogs leaped in',
Scuttling away through thick and thin,
To reach their dark asylums in the mud.
"Oh! oh!" said he, "then I can make them scud
As men make me; my presence scares

Some people too! Why, they're afraid of Hares!
I have alarmed the camp, you see.
Whence comes this courage? Tremble when I come?
I am a thunderbolt of war, may be;
My footfall dreadful as a battle drum!"

There's no poltroon, be sure, in any place,
But he can find a poltroon still more base.

The Two Pigeons

Two Pigeons once, as brother brother,
With true affection loved each other;
But one of them, foolishly, tired of home,
Resolved to distant lands to roam.
Then the other one said, with piteous tear,
"What! brother, and Would you then leave me here?
Of all the ills that on earth we share,
Absence from loved ones is bitterest woe!
And if to your heart this feeling's strange,
Let the dangers of travel your purpose change,
And, oh, at least for the spring-tide wait!
I heard a crow, on a neighboring tree,
Just now, predicting an awful fate
For some wretched bird; and I foresee
Falcons and snares awaiting thee.
What more can you want than what you've got—
A friend, a good dwelling, and wholesome cot?"
The other, by these pleadings shaken,
Almost had his whim forsaken;
But still, by restless ardor swayed,
Soon, in soothing tones, he said—
"Weep not, brother, I'll not stay
But for three short days away;
And then, quite satisfied, returning,
Impart to you my traveled learning.
Who stays at home has naught to say;
But I will have such things to tell,—
' 'Twas there I went,—It thus befell,'—
That you will think that you have been
In every action, every scene."
Thus having said, he bade adieu,

And forth on eager pinion flew;
But ere a dozen miles were past,
The skies, with clouds grew overcast
All drenched with rain the Pigeon sought
A tree, whose shelter was but naught;
And when, at length the rain was o'er,
His draggled wings could scarcely soar.
Soon after this, a field espying,
Whereon some grains of corn were lying,
He saw another Pigeon there,
And straight resolved to have his share.
So down he flies, and finds, too late,
The treacherous corn is only there
To tempt poor birds to hapless fate.
As the net was torn and old, however,
With beak, and claw, and fluttering wing,
And by despair's supreme endeavor,
He quickly broke string after string;
And, with the loss of half his Plumes,
Joyous, his flight once more resumes.
But cruel fate had yet in store
A sadder evil than before;
For, as our Pigeon slowly flew,
And bits of net behind him drew,
Like felon, just from prison 'scaped,
A hawk his course towards him shaped.
And now the Pigeon's life were ended,
But that, just then, with wings extended,
An eagle on the hawk descended.
Leaving the thieves to fight it out,
With beak and talon, helter-skelter,
The Pigeon 'neath a wall takes shelter;
And now believes, without a doubt,
That for the present time released,
The series of his woes has ceased.
But, lo! a cruel boy of ten
(That age knows not compassion's name),
Whirling his sling, with deadly aim,
Half kills the hapless bird, who then,
With splintered wing, half dead, and lame,
His zeal for travel deeply cursing,
Goes home to seek his brother's nursing.

By hook or by crook he hobbled along,
And arrived at home without further wrong.
Then, united once more, and safe from blows,
The brothers forgot their recent woes.

Oh, lover, happy lovers! never separate, I say,
But by the nearest rivulet your wandering footsteps stay.
Let each unto the other be a world that's ever fair,
Ever varied in its aspects, ever young and debonair.
Let each be dear to each, and as nothing count the rest.
I myself have sometimes been by a lover's ardor blest,
And then I'd not have changed for any palace here below,
Or for all that in the heavens in lustrous splendor glow,
The woods, and lanes, and fields, which were lightened by the eyes,
Which were gladdened by the feet of that shepherdess so fair,—
So sweet, and good, and young, to whom, bound by Cupid's ties,—
Fast bound, I thought, forever, I first breathed my oaths in air.
Alas! shall such sweet moments be never more for me?
Shall my restless soul no more on earth such tender objects see?
Oh, if I dared to venture on the lover's path again,
Should I still find sweet contentment in Cupid's broad domain?
Or is my heart grown torpid?—are my aspirations vain?

The Owl and the Mice

Whene'er you have a tale to tell,
Ne'er call it marvelous yourself,
If you would have it go down well,
For if you do, some spiteful elf
Will scorn it; but for once I'll vow
The tale that I shall tell you now
Is marvelous, and though like fable,
May be received as veritable.

So old a forest pine had grown,
At last 'twas marked to be cut down.
Within its branches' dark retreat
An Owl had made its gloomy seat—
The bird that Atropos thought meet
Its cry of vengeance to repeat.
Deep in this pine-tree's stem, time-worn,
With other living things forlorn,

Lived swarms of Mice, who had no toes;
But never Mice were fat as those,
For Master Owl, who'd snipped and torn,
Day after day fed them on corn.
The wise bird reasoned thus: "I've oft
Caught and stored Mice within my croft,
Which ran away, and 'scaped my claws;
One remedy is, I'll cut their paws,
And eat them slowly at my ease—
Now one of those, now one of these.
To eat them all at once were blameful,
And my digestion is so shameful."

You see the Owl was, in his way,
As wise as we; so, day by day,
His Mice had fit and due provision.
Yet, after this, some rash Cartesian
Is obstinate enough to swear
That Owls but mechanism are.
But how, then, could this night-bird find
This craftily-contrived device,
The nibbling of the paws of mice,
Were he not furnished with a mind?

See how he argued craftily
"Whene'er I catch these Mice, they flee;
And so the only way to save them
Is at one huge meal to brave them.
But that I cannot do; besides,
The wise man for bad days provides.
But how to keep them within reach?
Why, neatly bite the paws from each."
Now could there, gentle reader mine
Be human reasoning more fine?
Could Aristotle's self have wrought
A closer chain of argued thought?

Mother Goose Tales

BY CHARLES PERRAULT

Charles Perrault (1628–1703) the best-known writer/collector of European fairy tales in the early modern period, published his eight tales "Cinderella," "Sleeping Beauty," "Little Red Riding Hood," "Puss in Boots," "Tom Thumb," "The Fairies," "Ricky of the Tuft," and "Blue Beard" in 1697. Writing in his native French, Perrault always attached verse morals to his versions of these "Contes du temps passé" (Stories of past time). Although his collection is more purely the fairy tale genre, because his version of "Little Red Riding-Hood" has a typed animal character, a moral, and no magical or supernatural element, it shares traits with the fable, which is why it is included here.

Little Red Riding-Hood

Once upon a time, there lived in a certain village a little country girl, the prettiest creature ever seen. Her mother was excessively fond of her; and her grandmother doted on her much more. This good woman got made for her a little red riding-hood; which became the girl so extremely well that everybody called her Little Red Riding-Hood.

One day, her mother, having made some custards, said to her, "go, my dear, and see how thy Grand-Mamma does, for I hear she has been very ill, carry her a custard, and a little pot of butter." Little Red Riding-Hood set out immediately to go to her grandmother, who lived in another village. As she was going through the wood, she met with Gaffer Wolf, who had a very great mind to eat her up, but he durst not, because of some faggot-makers hard by in the forest.

He asked her whither she was going: The poor child, who did not know that it was dangerous to stay and hear a wolf talk, said to him, "I am going to see my Grand-Mamma, and carry her a custard, and a little pot of butter, from my mamma." "Does she live far off?" said the wolf. "Oh! ay," answered Little Red Riding-Hood, "it is beyond that mill you see there, at the first house in the village." "Well, said the wolf, and I'll go and see her too; I'll go this way, and go you that, and we shall see who will be there soonest."

The wolf began to run as fast as he could, taking the nearest way; and the little girl went by that farthest about, diverting herself gathering nuts, running after butterflies, and making nosegays of such little flowers as she met with. The wolf was not long before he got to the old woman's house. He knocked at the door, tap, tap. "Who's there?" "Your grandchild, Little Red Riding-Hood" (replied the wolf, counterfeiting her voice), "who has brought you a custard, and a little pot of butter, sent you by Mamma." The good grandmother, who was in bed, because she found herself somewhat ill, cried out "Pull the bobbin, and the latch will go up." The wolf pulled the bobbin and the door opened, and then presently he fell upon the good woman, and ate her up in a moment; for it was above three days that he had not touched a bit. He then shut the door, and went into the grandmother's bed, expecting Little Red Riding-Hood, who came some time afterwards and knocked at the door, tap, tap. "Who's there?" Little Red Riding-Hood, hearing the big voice of the wolf, was at first afraid, but believing her grandmother had got a cold, and was hoarse, answered, " 'Tis your grandchild, Little Red Riding-Hood, who has brought you a custard, and a little pot of butter Mamma sends you." The wolf cried out to her, softening his voice as much as he could, "Pull the bobbin, and the latch will go up." Little Red Riding-Hood pulled the bobbin, and the door opened.

The wolf, seeing her come in, said to her, hiding himself under the bedclothes, "Put the custard and the little pot of butter upon the stool, and come and lie down by me."

Little Red Riding-Hood undressed herself, and went into bed; where, being greatly amazed to see how her grandmother looked in her nightclothes, she said to her, "Grand-Mamma, what great arms you have got!" "That is the better to hug thee, my dear." "Grand-Mamma, what great legs you have got!" "That is to run the better, my child." "Grand-Mamma, what great ears you have got!" "That is to hear the better, my child." "Grand-Mamma, what great eyes you have got!" "That is to see the better, my child." "Grand-Mamma, what great teeth you have got!" "That is to eat thee up." And saying these words, this wicked wolf fell upon poor Little Red Riding-Hood, and ate her all up.

The Moral

From this short story easy we discern,
What conduct all young people ought to learn.
But above all, young growing misses fair,
Whose orient rosy blooms begin t'appear:
Who, beauties in the fragrant spring of age,
With pretty airs young hearts are apt t'engage,
Ill do they listen to all sorts of tongues,
Since some enchant and lure like Sirens' songs.
No wonder therefore, 'tis, if overpower'd,
So many of them has the wolf devour'd.
The wolf, I say, for wolves too sure there are
Of every sort, and every character.
Some of them mild and gentle humor'd be,
Of noise and gall, and rancour wholly free;
Who tame, familiar, full of complaisance,
Ogle and leer, languish, cajole and glance;
With luring tongues, and language wond'rous sweet,
Follow young ladies as they walk the street,
Ev'n to their very houses, nay, beside,
And artful, tho' their true designs they hide:
Yet ah! these simpering wolves, who does not see,
Most dang'rous of all wolves in fact they be?

The Fable of the Bees

by Bernard Mandeville

Bernard Mandeville (1670–1733), a native of Holland, moved to England in the early 1690s "to learn the language." By 1703, his English was certainly good enough to publish *Some Fables After the Easie and Familiar Method of Monsieur de la Fontaine, followed by Aesop Dress'd or a Collection of Fables Writ in Familiar Verse.* But his magnum opus remains *The Fable of the Bees, or Private Vices, Publick Benefits,* which begins as an 18-page verse allegory published in 1705, titled "The Grumbling Hive: or, Knaves turn'd Honest," followed by a page-long "Moral" reprinted here. The sequel to this is an 800-page compendium of philosophical reflections and commentary. Over the next 24 years, Mandeville expanded the text of the fable with hundreds of pages of commentary on the potential value of individual greed and selfishness if they worked to the common good of the social whole. As such, Mandeville's case is that of a writer of fables whose production led him to become one of the prime ethical and political thinkers of the early Enlightenment. The resulting ethical question of deciding the relation between partial evil and general good becomes a pervasive topic of discussion in the works of such diverse figures as Alexander Pope, Adam Smith, and Karl Marx. The "Moral" reprinted here is a verse commentary on the bees' behavior in "The Grumbling Hive."

The Moral

from "The Grumbling Hive: or, Knaves Turn'd Honest."

Then leave Complaints: Fools only strive
To make a Great and Honest Hive
T'enjoy the World's Conveniences,

Be fam'd in War, yet live in Ease,
Without Great Vices, is a vain
Eutopia seated in the Brain.
Fraud, Luxury and Pride must live
While we the Benefits receive:
Hunger's a dreadful Plague, no doubt,
Yet who digests or thrives without?
Do we not owe the Growth of Wine
To the dry shabby crooked Vine?
Which, while its Shoots neglected stood,
Chok'd other Plants, and ran to Wood;
But blest us with its noble Fruit,
As soon as it was ty'd and cut:
So Vice is beneficial found,
When it's by Justice lopt and bound;
Nay, where the people would be great,
As necessary to the State,
As Hunger is to make 'em eat.
Bare virtue can't make Nations live
In Splendor; they, that would revive
A Golden Age, must be as free,
For acorns, as for Honesty.

Fables and Epigrams

BY G. E. LESSING

Gotthold Ephraim Lessing (1729–1781), German playwright and critic, believed in the importance of assuring a formal unity between fable narrative and moral lesson. While some fabulists exploit the possible dissonance, or even contradictions, between the two, Lessing sought to subordinate storytelling to the didacticism of the moral.

The Raven and the Fox

A raven bore away in his talons a poisoned piece of meat, which an angry gardener had provided for certain annoying rats. Perched on an old oak tree, he was just ready to devour it, when a fox appeared beneath, and exclaimed, "Heaven bless you, bird of Jupiter!"

"For whom do you take me?" asked the raven.

"For whom do I take you?" rejoined the fox. "Are you not the stately eagle which daily descends from the right hand of Jupiter to this oak tree, to feed me, the poor fox? Why would you conceal yourself? Do I not behold in your victorious claw the prayed-for gift which Jupiter continues to send through you?"

The raven was surprised, and felt an inward pleasure at being mistaken for an eagle. "I must not undeceive the fox," said he to himself, and stupidly dropping his prey, he proudly flew away. The fox received the prize with a grin, and devoured it with malignant joy. That joy, however, was soon turned into sorrow; the poison operated, and he died.

Abominable flatterers! Would that you were all thus rewarded with one poison for another!

The Man and the Dog

A man was bitten by a dog, flew into a passion and killed it. The wound appearing dangerous, a surgeon was deemed necessary. "I am not acquainted with a better remedy," said the latter, "than that of dipping a piece of bread in the wound, and causing the mischievous dog to eat it. If that sympathetic prescription avail not, then"—here the surgeon shrugged up his shoulders—"O, fatal anger," exclaimed the man, "I have killed the dog!"

The Sick Wolf

The wolf being at the point of death, cast a retrospective glance on his past life. "I am certainly a sinner," he plaintively observed, "but, I trust, not one of the greatest. I have doubtless committed evil; but I have also done much good. I remember that once when a lamb, which had strayed from the flock, came so near me, I might have devoured it with the greatest ease; I forbore to do so. About the same time I listened to the abuse of an angry sheep with the most edifying indifference, although no watchdog was to be feared."

"To all this I can bear witness," said the fox, who was assisting his ghostly preparations. "I recollect all the particulars. It was just at the time you suffered so much from the bone in your throat."

Fables

BY IVAN KRYLOV

Ivan Krylov (1768–1844) is often called the La Fontaine of Russia, but like other fabulists, his "translations" of his French counterpart soon depart from their Gallic source and inspire a whole new set of homespun fables. The virtues of the underdog are reflected throughout his fables along with a deep appreciation of the common folk, i.e. the Russian peasants, and the horrors they endured during the Napoleonic invasion.

The Wolf in the Kennel

A wolf, one night, thinking to climb into a sheepfold, fell into a kennel. Immediately the whole kennel was up in arms. The dogs, scenting the grisly disturber so near at hand, began to bark in their quarters, and to tear out to the fight.

"Hallo, lads, a thief!" cried the keepers; and immediately the gates were shut. In a moment the kennel became a hell. Men came running, one armed with a club, another with a gun. "Lights!" they cry; "bring lights!" The lights being brought, our Wolf is seen sitting squeezed up in the furthest corner, gnashing its teeth, its hide bristling, and its eyes looking as if it would fain eat up the whole party. Seeing, however, that it is not now in the presence of the flock, and that it is now called upon to pay the penalty for the sheep it has killed, my trickster resorts to negotiation, beginning thus:

"Friends, what is all this fuss about? I am your ancient gossip and comrade; and I have come here to contract an alliance with you—not with the slightest intention of quarrelling. Let us forget the past, and declare in favor of mutual harmony. Not only will I for the future avoid touching the flocks belonging to this spot, but I will gladly fight in their behalf against others; and I swear on the word of a Wolf that I —"

"Listen, neighbor," here interrupted the huntsman. "You are gray-coated; but I, friend, am gray-headed, and I have long known what your wolfish natures are like, and therefore it is my custom never to make peace with wolves until I have torn their skin from off their backs."

With that he let go the pack of hounds on the Wolf.

The Pike and the Cat

A conceited Pike took it into its head to exercise the functions of a cat. I do not know whether the Evil One had plagued it with envy, or whether, perhaps, it had grown tired of fishy fare; but, at all events, it thought fit to ask the cat to take it out to the chase, with the intention of catching a few mice in the warehouse. "But, my dear friend," Vaska says to the Pike, "do you understand that kind of work? Take care, gossip, that you don't incur disgrace. It isn't without reason that they say, 'The work ought to be in the master's power.' "

"Why really, gossip, what a tremendous affair it is! Mice, indeed! Why, I have been in the habit of catching perches!"

"Oh, very well. Come along!"

They went; they lay each in ambush. The Cat thoroughly enjoyed itself; made a hearty meal; then went to look after its comrade. Alas! The Pike, almost destitute of life, lay there gasping, its tail nibbled away by the mice. So the Cat seeing its comrade had undertaken a task quite beyond its strength, dragged it back, half dead, to its pond.

The Eagle and the Spider

An eagle had soared above the clouds to the loftiest peak of the Caucasus. There, on an ancient cedar it settled, and admired the landscape visible at its feet. It seemed as if the borders of the world could be seen from thence. Here flowed rivers, winding across the plains; there stood woods and meadows, adorned with the full garb of spring; and, beyond, frowned the angry Caspian Sea, black as a raven's wing.

"Praise be to thee, o Jove, that, as ruler of the world, thou hast bestowed on me such powers of flight that I know of no heights to me inaccessible!"—thus the Eagle addressed Jupiter—"insomuch that I now look upon the beauties of the world from a point whither no other being has ever flown."

"What a boaster you are!" replies a Spider to it from a twig. "As I sit here, am I lower than you, comrade?"

The Eagle looks up. Truly enough, the Spider is busy spinning its web about a twig overhead, just as if it wanted to shut out the sunlight from the Eagle.

"How did you get up to this height?" asks the Eagle. "Even among the strongest of wing there are some who would not dare to trust themselves here. But you, weak and wingless, is it possible you can have crawled here?"

"No; I didn't use that means of rising aloft."

"Well, then, how did you get here?"

"Why, I just fastened myself on to you, and you brought me yourself from down below on your tail-feathers. But I know how to maintain my position here without your help, so I beg you will not assume such airs in my presence; for know that I—"

At this moment a gust of wind comes suddenly flying by, and whirls away the spider again into the lowest depths.

The Ant

A certain Ant had extraordinary strength, such as had never been heard of even in the days of old. It could even, as its trustworthy historian states, lift up two large grains of barley at once! Besides this, it was also remarkable for wonderful courage. Whenever it saw a worm, it immediately stuck its claws into it, and it would even go alone against a spider. And so it acquired such a reputation on its anthill, that it became the sole subject of conversation.

Extravagant praise I consider poison; but our ant was not of the same opinion: it delighted in it, measured it by its own conceit, and believed the whole of it. At length its head became so turned that it determined to exhibit itself to the neighboring city, that it might acquire fame by showing off its strength there.

Perched on the top of a lofty cartload of hay, having proudly made its way to the side of the moujik in charge, it enters the city in great state. But, alas! What a blow to its pride! It had imagined that the whole bazaar would run together to see it, as to a fire. But not a word is said about it, every one being absorbed in his own business. Our Ant seizes a leaf, and jerks it about, tumbles down, leaps up again. Still not a soul pays it any attention. At last, wearied with exerting itself, and holding itself proudly erect, it says, with vexation, to Barbos, the mastiff, lying beside its master's cart, "It must be confessed, mustn't it, that the people of your city have neither eyes nor brains? Can it really be true that no one remarks me, although I have been straining myself here for a whole hour? And yet I'm sure that at home I am well known to the whole of the anthill."

And so it went back again, utterly crestfallen.

The Wolves and the Sheep

The Sheep could not live in peace on account of the Wolves, and the evil increased to such a pitch, that at last the rulers of the beasts had to take vigorous steps towards interfering and saving the victims. With that intent a council was summoned. The majority of its members, it is true, were Wolves; but then all Wolves are not badly spoken of. There have been Wolves known, and that often (such instances are never forgotten), to have walked past a flock quite peacefully – when completely gorged. So why should not Wolves have seats in the council? Although it was necessary to protect the Sheep, yet there was no reason for utterly suppressing the Wolves.

Well, the meeting took place in the thick wood. They pondered, considered, harangued, and at last framed a decree. Here you have it, word for word: — "As soon as a Wolf shall have disturbed a flock, and shall have begun to worry a Sheep, then the Sheep shall be allowed, without respect to persons, to seize it by the scruf of the neck, to carry it into the nearest thicket or wood, and there to bring it before the court."

This law is everything that can be desired. Only, I have remarked, up to the present day, that although the Wolves are not to be allowed to worry with impunity, yet in all cases, whether the Sheep be plaintiff or defendant, the Wolf is always sure, in spite of all opposition, to carry off the Sheep into the forest.

Uncle Remus

by Joel Chandler Harris

Joel Chandler Harris (1848–1908) was a white writer for the *Atlanta Constitution* during the post–Civil War years. Although Uncle Remus is fictitious, his stories reflect the author's recollection of a white childhood in the South before the Civil War. As such, they recall the slave culture and the fable tradition of African Americans still influenced by the fable tradition that they had brought with them from Africa. Harris' work, however, reflects both nostalgia for an earlier South and hope that centuries of oppression could be overcome.

Uncle Remus Initiates the Little Boy

One evening recently, the lady whom Uncle Remus calls "Miss Sally" missed her little seven-year-old boy. Making search for him through the house and through the yard, she heard the sound of voices in the old man's cabin, and, looking through the window, saw the child sitting by Uncle Remus. His head rested against the old man's arm, and he was gazing with an expression of the most intense interest into the rough, weather-beaten face, that beamed so kindly upon him. This is what "Miss Sally" heard:

"Bimeby, one day, arter Brer Fox bin doin' all dat he could fer ter ketch Brer Rabbit, en Brer Rabbit bin doin' all he could fer to keep 'im fum it, Brer Fox say to hisse'f dat he'd put up a game on Brer Rabbit, en he ain't mo'n got de wuds out'n his mouf twel Brer Rabbit come a lopin' up de big road, lookin' des ez plump, en ez fat, en ez sassy ez a Moggin boss in a barley-patch.

" 'Hol' on dar, Brer Rabbit,' sez Brer Fox, sezee.

" 'I ain't got time, Brer Fox,' sez Brer Rabbit, sezee, sorter mendin' his licks.

" 'I wanter have some confab wid you, Brer Rabbit,' sez Brer Fox, sezee.

" 'All right, Brer Fox, but you better holler fum whar you stan'. I'm monstus full er fleas dis mawnin',' sez Brer Rabbit, sezee.

" 'I seed Brer B'ar yistiddy,' sez Brer Fox, sezee, 'en he sorter rake me over de coals kaze you en me ain't make frens en live naberly, en I told 'im dat I'd see you.'

"Den Brer Rabbit scratch one year wid his off hinefoot sorter jub'usly, en den he ups en sez, sezee:

" 'All a settin', Brer Fox. Spose'n you drap roun' ter-morrer en take dinner wid me. We ain't got no great doin's at our house, but I speck de old 'oman en de chilluns kin sorter scramble roun' en git up sump'n fer ter stay yo'stummuck.'

" 'I'm 'gree'ble, Brer Rabbit,' sez Brer Fox, sezee.

" 'Den I'll 'pen' on you,' sez Brer Rabbit, sezee.

"Nex' day, Mr. Rabbit an' Miss Rabbit got up soon, 'fo' day, en raided on a gyarden like Miss Sally's out dar, en got some cabbiges en some roas'n years, en some sparrer-grass, en dey fix up a smashin' dinner. Bimeby one er de little Rabbits, playin' out in de backyard, come runnin' in hollerin', 'Oh, ma! oh, ma! I seed Mr. Fox a comin'!' En den Brer Rabbit he tuck de chilluns by der years en make um set down, en den him and Miss Rabbit sorter dally roun' waitin' for Brer Fox. En dey keep on waitin', but no Brer Fox ain't come. Atter 'while Brer Rabbit goes to de do', easy like, en peep out, en dar, stickin' fum behime de cornder, wuz de tip-een'er Brer Fox tail. Den Brer Rabbit shot de do' en sot down, en put his paws behime his years en begin fer ter sing:

" 'De place wharbouts you spill de grease,
Right dar youer boun' ter slide,
An' whar you fine a bunch er ha'r,
You'll sholy fine de hide.'

"Nex' day, Brer Fox sont word by Mr. Mink, en skuze hisse'f kaze he wuz too sick fer ter come, en he ax Brer Rabbit fer to come en take dinner wid him, en Brer Rabbit say he wuz 'gree'ble.

"Bimeby, w'en de shadders wuz at der shortes', Brer Rabbit he sorter brush up en santer down ter Brer Fox's house, en w'en he got dar, he hear somebody groanin', en he look in de do' en dar he see Brer Fox settin' up in a rockin' cheer all wrop up wid flannil, en he look mighty weak. Brer Rabbit look all 'roun', he did, but he ain't see no dinner. De dishpan wuz settin' on de table, en close by wuz a kyarvin' knife.

" 'Look like you gwineter have chicken fer dinner, Brer Fox,' sez Brer Rabbit, sezee.

" 'Yes, Brer Rabbit, deyer nice, en fresh, en tender,' sez Brer Fox, sezee.

"Den Brer Rabbit sorter pull his mustarsh, en say: 'You ain't got no calamus root, is you, Brer Fox? I done got so now dat I can't eat no chicken 'ceppin she's seasoned up wid calamus root.' En wid dat Brer Rabbit lipt out er de do' and dodge 'mong de bushes, en sot dar watchin' fer Brer Fox; en he ain't watch long, nudder, kaze Brer Fox flung off de flannil en crope out er de house en got whar he could cloze in on Brer Rabbit, en bimeby Brer Rabbit holler out: 'Oh, Brer Fox! I'll des put yo' calamus root out yer on dish yer stump. Better come git it while hit's fresh,' and wid dat Brer Rabbit gallop off home. En Brer Fox ain't never kotch 'im yit, en wa't's mo', honey, he ain't gwineter."

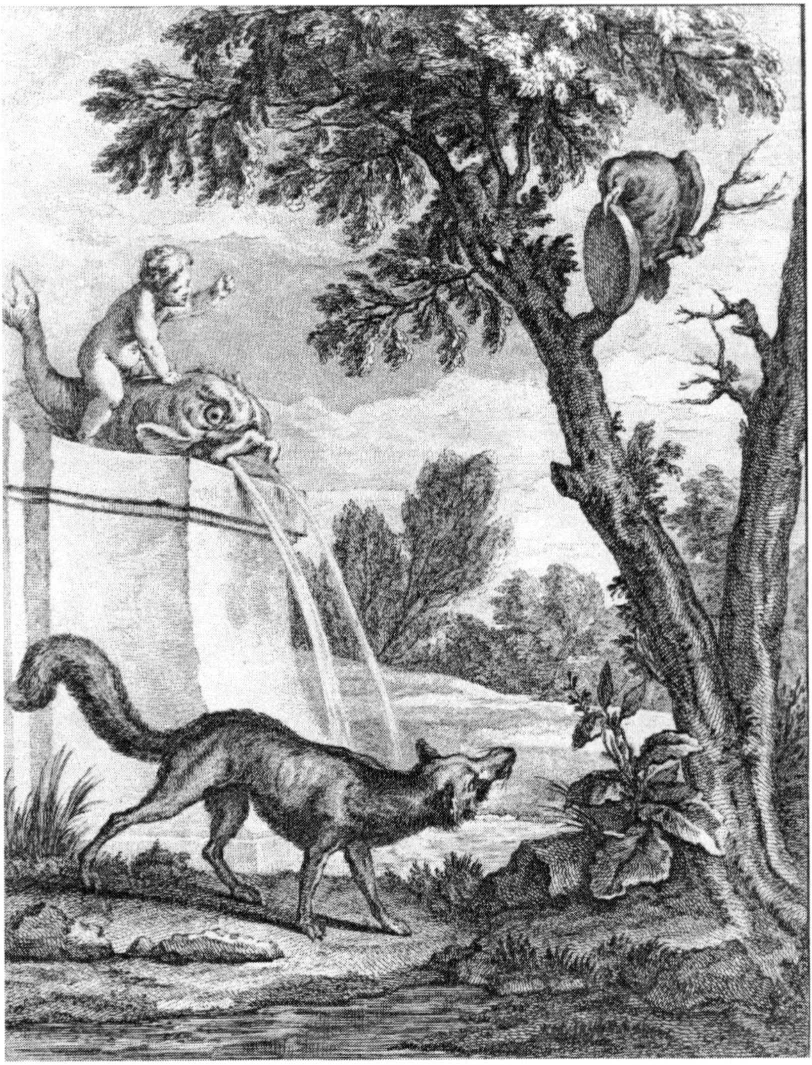

Cric? Crac! Fables Créoles

BY GEORGES SYLVAIN

Georges Sylvain (1866–1925), was a Haitian writer who "translated" La Fontaine's fables into Creole, but like La Fontaine's translations of Aesop and others, Sylvain transforms his predecessor's fables into a powerful critique of the French colonial legacy while reconnecting them to African storytelling traditions. The title of his collection, *Cric? Crac!* (1901) refers to the rhetorical question and answer between storyteller and listener that inaugurates the narration.

Crow and Fox

Let me tell you today about
Two animals from France:
Crow and then Fox.
Crow, that bird who's
Always serious, like a loaf of stale bread.
The way he looks, you'd say
He was one of those young folks that write for magazines.
More exactly, to know a devil in mourning clothes
Is to know him.
Brother Fox, on the other hand,
He's family with the dog; alive as the air.
As hip as a master at arms. Of
All the animals on earth, he's the one
Who plays the little mischief-maker—Bouqui
He's the jackass, everybody knows that!
(Cric? Crac! No way out up above, no way out down below!
Hey kids! If they call me,
Tell me to go on a bit more! . . .)

Okay! . . . Doc Crow, early one morning,
Was perched up on a pine tree.
In his mouth, a chunk of Gruyère cheese
That he'd just picked up along the docks.
                    All ready to eat,
You'd think by his face he'd be all chilled?
                    Him? No way!
His kind of folks would rather be dead
                    Than laugh!
White folks say the more the cheese smells,
The better it is. Crow's cheese
Must have been the king of all cheeses; just the smell—yeah!
Was enough to make his hunger go away.
Brother Fox was passing by,
He took just one whiff of that Gruyère
And the brother came to a stop;
He said: "What the . . . !" and then
Started to drool.
So what did he do? (Listen, yeah!) Acting like
He hadn't seen anybody yet, the Brother
Raised his eyes up high
And said: "Oh, hi Doc,"
"How you been doing? Okay, thank you! . . ."
"Hey those are some cool threads our Doc is wearing,
"No jiving! That's real fine,
"Made in Paris, hunh?
"Fashion, style, cut,
"It's chic all the way!
"Oh yeah! You've outdone yourself this time!
"And you're just the right size to wear it! And now,
"They tell me you're a musician too.
"Everywhere, all they talk about is you.
"How good looking you are, how well you sing!
"But when they're talking, my mouth stays shut.
"I haven't yet had a chance to hear you sing!
"But if what folks say is true,
"Well, you'd have to reckon that the good God's no longer
the good God
"For letting one of his creatures get all the goods."
And all the while Fox was talking,
(They've got the old soft jaw, those slick fellahs!)
Doc Crow had a certain way
Of shifting his shoulders, as if to say:

"Ow! Ow! Ow!" Never mind that deep down
His nostrils began to flare with the desire
To show that he really did know how to sing.
Our Doc opened his beak up as wide as he could
Just like he'd seen in Church at choir time.
(Blip!) The cheese fell out.
It never even made it to the ground:
Fox was waiting there, open mouthed, ready to go.
Seeing it fall, he caught it, put
His two paws on it,
And then spoke to Crow like this:
"Hey man, I was just joking, yeah!
"When did you ever know how to sing?
"Your voice sounds like a cracked old pot.
"And as for that lame cod-tailed suit,
"You strut about in,
"It was put together down at Bro' Pierre's.
"That little bit of cheese
"Was the best thing you had.
"Thanks, my sweet! How it tasted
"I'll tell you some other day."
That said, he turned his back on him.
And Doc Crow just stood there looking dumb.

Too bad for those who don't know
With what food parasites fatten themselves!
Those who know how to read books may think they are great scholars.
The grass don't grow out on the highways:
The mind's what leads the body!

—*Translated by Georges Van Den Abbeele*

The Bird Who Cleans the World and Other Mayan Fables

BY VICTOR MONTEJO

Victor Montejo (born 1951) is a contemporary Mayan writer, scholar, and activist whose retrieval of indigenous Mayan fables also lets them speak to contemporary issues of poverty, exploitation, and migration. The fables in this collection originate among the Jakaltek Mayans and were told to the author by his mother and the elders of the Mayan region. Victor Montejo is a professor of Native American Studies at the University of California, Davis.

The Snail and the Minnow

A lordly snail, forgetting his limitations, challenged a bold minnow to a race.

"Very good," the minnow replied. "We will run the course you want, but the race must have its rules and a prize for the winner."

"I will put up my sombrero!" the snail said without thinking and having nothing else to offer. And so they made their deal.

The minnow swam round and round in the river while the snail tried his best to start the race. What happened then? Well, just what had to happen. The lordly snail lost his sombrero!

The War of the Wasps

One day a cricket, wanting rest for the night, arrived in the jaguar's cave. Without the consent or even the knowledge of the mansion's owners, he climbed into a little crevice. From there, as is the custom or the vice of this kind, he began to chirp in the middle of the night, disturbing the holy peace and irritating the big family of carnivores.

The chirping of the cricket infuriated the residents of the cave and was heard for a great distance, tearing the silence of the night and disturbing their sleep. After several hours had passed the jaguars (*b'alam*) could bear the scandalous chirping no more. They got up with the clear intention of exterminating the source of that disagreeable music.

They clawed at the walls on all sides of the caves looking for the source of their misery, but the night was too dark, and the cricket had hidden himself in the highest and darkest crevice.

When dawn came, the jaguars got up in a bad mood and watched for the unknown visitor who had kept them up all night. The cricket took one hop and revealed himself. The jaguars were very puzzled to see how small a musician had annoyed them so much.

"Come down from there," they demanded.

The cricket remained where he was near his hiding place. If he came down, he surely would never again serenade the peaceful night. So, fearing the great danger below, he did not move.

The jaguars insisted again. "Come down and take what you deserve."

Then the cricket quickly looked for some safe way to escape. He said very seriously, "What a shame! You who are called 'King of the Animals' want to do away with a simple defenseless evening troubadour who only wants to celebrate love in his songs. You do not deserve your noble title."

The jaguars felt insulted and replied, "Then call whomever you want to help you, because you are not going to humiliate us before anything or anybody."

The cricket answered, "If I call other insects to defend me, I am sure that we will triumph. But my wish is that there be peace and tranquility among us all."

"How can some simple insects conquer us, we who are the strongest of the animals?" roared the jaguars. "Eah! Let them all come to defend you, and we'll wait here among our own kind with claws and fangs."

A rabbit who was listening to the discussion set out to help the cricket. Quickly he went through the forest carrying large hollow gourds, looking for all kinds of wasps. The wasps all agreed to help the cricket. So with all the venom stored in their stingers, they climbed into the gourds to be carried to where the event would take place.

The jaguars, too, were calling other animals to their side. They gathered the largest and most ferocious, like the pumas, the mountain cats, and the wild boars. They all gathered on the grassy plain where the cricket approached them to say that everyone was ready. The jaguars, hearing that their opponents were ready, threw themselves forward furiously, roaring and causing a great panic among the other inhabitants of the forest.

The rabbit waited for an opportune moment. When he thought the time was right, he uncovered the big gourds and let loose a torrent of furious wasps who went after the bodies of their enemies, where they buried their stingers. The ferocious beasts were covered with stinging wasps, and no matter how much they roared, ran and shook themselves, they couldn't get rid of their attackers. Each time, the wasps stung more furiously, injecting their poison in the eyes, the noses, the tails, and everywhere, tormenting the jaguars horribly. Tired of fighting in vain, the jaguars rolled on the ground trying to free themselves of their tireless persecutors. It is hard to believe, but so it was that the cricket, with help from the rabbit and the wasps, succeeded in conquering so easily the fearsome jaguars who ran away in all directions seeking refuge and salvation in their caves and under the bushes.

The King of the Animals

The jaguar (*b'alam*) and the mountain lion (*kaqkoh*) sent a declaration throughout the jungle. "Let all the animals come together, from the greatest to the smallest without exception, to elect the king of the animals." The citizens faced a delicate decision—to elect their delegates proudly. All the citizens of the jungle had arrived from even the most secret places. Shouting and cheering, they supported their favorite. The animals came from everywhere to debate the merits of the contenders. The jungle shook with the clamor.

The lion remained calm. The jaguar, however, was pacing nervously, even wildly, among the crowds, assuring himself that everyone was present. Suddenly he said, "One is missing, the rabbit!"

So it was. The rabbit was the only animal who had not come at the appointed time.

"The election is a tie and we need the rabbit to decide," said the jaguar. "I'll go get him whether it's for better or for worse."

This jaguar wanted to win by any means. He didn't take long to find the rabbit, who was sleeping beneath some green fronds. Very diplomatically he asked, "What's up, my fine friend? You haven't come to the election. After all, you are he who performs great deeds and makes great decisions. Now you are absent when we need you most."

"Oh, I'm very sorry, Señor Jaguar. I am very sick and I can't get up from my cot. Perhaps you would like to carry me on your back." The clever rabbit looked very sick and held a wad of bean leaves to his head.

Climb on my back and we will be off, since everyone is waiting for us." The jaguar loaded the sick-looking rabbit on his back and soon they arrived at the field where the election was to be decided.

"The rabbit has arrived! The wise rabbit has arrived," everyone shouted at once. The jaguar stepped to one side twitching his enormous tail while he awaited the decisive vote from the rabbit.

The rabbit was quick to speak up. "One moment, friends. Before we arrive at such an important decision, it is wise to get to know the candidates more thoroughly. So let's see. The jaguar seems a good candidate because he is so agile, and with such claws he is a good hunter. But for this very reason he is a serious danger to all of us. As king he would have complete liberty to exterminate us in order to satisfy his ever-voracious appetite. Now the lion is a little more peaceful and less impulsive than the jaguar. For this reason I vote for the lion as our king!"

All the other animals seconded the rabbit's wise decision. And so the mountain lion was confirmed the king of the jungle. The jaguar went away defeated. He had learned that the person who has his ideals and principles well-guarded cannot be easily corrupted, even if you carry him a long way.

The Rabbit and the Goat (short version)

Tired of living a poor and miserable life, one day a rabbit decided to abandon his homeland and venture to a distant and unknown place. After walking a great distance, the rabbit stopped under the shade of a bush. He was about to lie down and rest when he heard a noise on the ground, not too far away. It was a horse that was grazing quietly on the prairie and kicking the ground in an effort to repel the flies on his back. The rabbit approached the horse slowly and said. "How come, as big as you are, you allow yourself to be tied there to that post without the freedom to roam wherever you please? Learn from me. Despite being very small, I am free to seek adventure. If you want to follow me, I can untie you right now." After meditating for a while, the horse replied, "It is a good proposal, Mister Adventurer, but I have a master and I must stay here where he left me. I am used to this place, so I cannot follow you, Mister Rabbit."

The rabbit continued on his way and soon he arrived where an ox was tied to a post. The rabbit approached the animal and invited him to travel in search of a better place to live. "Hey, Mister Ox, how come you, being so big, are there tied to a post without freedom to travel? Join me, I am going to a rich and beautiful country where life is easy." The ox replied: "No, Mister Rabbit, this is the place where I have lived and I don't want to abandon it. Go on your way, because my master will appear with his dogs and then you will be in trouble."

The rabbit continued his adventure alone. Day after day he walked under the heat of the sun, until he got very tired. He then decided to rest under some green bushes. Once again, he was about to rest when he heard the bleating of sheep and goats not far from there. Rabbit approached the fence where the animals were congregated and said. "Hello, my friends, I am so saddened to see you in this prison. I can only offer myself to free you, if you want to follow me to the *porisal*. The sheep asked what the *porisal* was, and the rabbit explained. "The *porisal* is a marvelous place where there is money and life is easy. I don't even know where this place is, but I am eager to travel to find it and enjoy it. People say that it is truly a paradise where very few people have traveled."

All the sheep and goats were about to be convinced, but then the oldest of the rams said. "Stop, Mister. Don't try to deceive us; we are tired of being deceived with lies and tricks." The rabbit continued describing the wonderful place he was searching for, and finally someone agreed to accompany him. This was an adult goat who said: "Me sir, I would like to follow you, if it is true that there is a better place than this one where I am living." The rabbit wasted no time in helping the goat escape from the fence. They walked and walked for a long time until the rabbit started to limp. Then, finding a little clearing in the forest, the rabbit lay down on the ground and started to cry out as if he were very sick. The goat, worried about his companion, asked: "What's wrong, dear friend Rabbit?" The rabbit responded in a tremulous voice. "Oh, dear friend, I am dying, I am dying!" "What can I do for you? How can I help you get well?" asked the goat worriedly. Hearing the compassionate voice of his companion, the rabbit said. "I may get better if you carry me on your back and continue the trip. Now, I cannot move and I may die right here if you don't help me." The goat agreed to carry the supposedly sick rabbit on his back. The goat walked for many days, carrying the rabbit on his back. When the goat could not run faster, the rabbit started to whip him with a twig, as if he were a cowboy. "Hurry up; you're going too slow," said the rabbit, hitting the goat once again. Then the goat realized he was being used by the rabbit and stopped suddenly. "It seems you are already healthy; that's why you can now hit me with all your strength. I ask you to get off my back right now," said the goat. The rabbit tried his tricks once again. "Oh, Friend Goat, my bones are still hurting and I cannot walk." "Your bones will hurt even more if you don't get down off my back right now," commanded the goat. The rabbit was stubborn, so the goat began jumping and kicking around like a wild stallion, until the poor rabbit flew off his back and landed on the gravel. The rabbit cried out "ouch!" when he hit his head on the hard ground. "This is what you deserve, you liar. And stop deceiving and tricking the peaceful inhabitants of the forest."

After this fight, both of them realized that it was too late to continue walking, so they decided to find a place to rest and spend the night. Somehow they realized they were close to their final destination. They looked around and found a cave where three jaguar cubs were playing. "I'm scared," said the goat, retreating, ready to run for his life. The rabbit stopped him and said. "Don't worry my friend, they are only little kittens. Besides, we have to have courage to cross this land, since we have already suffered a lot to get to this point." Then, the rabbit asked the playful cubs. "Eh, children, where is your mother?" The little cubs answered without paying attention to the intruders. "She went to find food for us, and she will be back soon."

The goat began to feel fear again. Then the rabbit told the cubs. "We will spend the night here, near you. Since we don't want to bother you, we will hide high up in the crevices of the cavern. Don't tell your mother that we are staying at the borders of her domain."

"She has a good nose and she will soon find you," said the mischievous cubs. The rabbit did not care, so he and the goat moved to another hidden section of the cave, up above the ground. The goat got scared hearing the noises down below. They truly were at the edge of a well-protected and dangerous territory. "Don't worry, venturing into a new land always has its good and bad sides," said the rabbit.

It was already dark when they heard the roaring of the mother jaguar and others who came to sleep in the cave. "Owiyyuuuu, grrrrr...!" The mother jaguar stopped abruptly when she smelled the ground where the visitors had stood. "Did anybody come to the cave when I was away?" asked the jaguar.

The cubs responded by showing their mother the crevice where the two travelers had hidden, hoping to pass through the land patrolled by the jaguars. The cubs said, "Two travelers passed by. One was big and the other small. They invaded our house while you were away." Trembling with fear in the crevice high above and at the edge of a big hole in the cave, the goat began to cry. "My friend rabbit, I'm in big trouble, I gotta pee, real bad!"

The rabbit scolded the goat. "You cannot do that right now, the jaguars will discover our hiding place and capture us."

"I cannot resist, Friend Rabbit. I need to pee immediately, or I'm going to explode," insisted the goat.

"Okay, lie down on the rock, but on your back, so you can pee through your fur without making any noise." The goat obeyed the rabbit and lay down on his back. While the goat was peeing, the jaguar growled and the poor goat tried to stand up, but he slid across the wet rock and fell into the big hole in the cave. The rabbit and the jaguar heard the noise of the goat's body hitting the rocks as he fell into the hole. The rabbit began to shout at the unfortunate goat. "Hold on, hold on!" The rabbit tried to create confusion so the jaguar would think there were other bigger animals up there. The mother jaguar started to flee the cave with her cubs, but then she decided to stay. Why should I run away? This is my territory and I have to defend it. I won't let other animals pass by, since I don't want strangers to share this territory with me and those of my kind. The jaguar went inside the cave and began searching for the one that was shouting noisily "Hold on, hold on!" The rabbit managed to hide himself and waited until the jaguar went down into the hole to see who was the unfortunate one who had fallen. At the bottom of the hole was the poor goat, dead. The jaguar brought it up to her cubs and the other jaguars, and they ate it ravenously. Meanwhile, the rabbit managed to cross the borderland of the jaguars and continued his adventure in search of the *porisal,* or the place of opportunity, the paradise where there were riches and life is easy and food plentiful.

Native North American Fables

BY BARRY LOPEZ

The following versions are by Barry Lopez (born 1945), author of *Arctic Dreams*, from his collection *Giving Birth to Thunder, Sleeping With His Daughter: Coyote Builds North America*.

Coyote and Spider

One day Coyote was coming along. He was very hungry. Spider was on a tree. Coyote found Spider and wanted to eat him.

"What are you trying to do?" said Spider.

"I am going to eat you."

"You know, I heard some people over there talking about killing you. I'll go over there and find out what they are going to do."

"All right," said Coyote. "Come back soon."

Spider promised he would, but he did not return.

Coyote went on and found another spider. He was going to eat him.

"Now, I'll tell you something good," said Spider. "Why do you think I am on this tree? What do you think of this?"

"I don't know."

"I hold on to this tree, shut my eyes for a short time and see everything all over the world. This tree is chief of the whole world, that is why spiders always go on trees."

"That is new to me," said Coyote.

"Don't you wish to see everything?"

"Yes."

"Well, shut your eyes for a while, hold on to this tree, and you will see everything."

As soon as Coyote had closed his eyes, Spider went away. Coyote never saw anything. That is how it was with him.

Coyote Imitates Mountain Lion

Coyote was going along and he saw a rock rolling down the hill. It rolled down toward some deer and they jumped. Coyote wondered who was rolling stones and looked up at the top of the hill. Another stone came rolling down past Coyote toward the deer and the deer jumped again. Then a third stone came down and the deer jumped only a little. They knew it was only a stone.

The next moment another stone came by Coyote. But this was a soft rock. It was Mountain Lion who had rolled himself up like a rock and was rolling down the hill.

"What a funny rock," thought Coyote. "It doesn't make any noise when it rolls."

Mountain Lion rolled right up to the deer, who were not suspicious of the rolling rocks by this time. Then Coyote saw Mountain Lion get up, jump on a big deer and kill it. Mountain Lion picked up the deer and carried it up to a cliff where he could eat it and see the country all around. The rest of the deer ran off around the hill.

Coyote thought this would be a good way to get deer.

He rolled a stone down the hill to where the deer were and they jumped. He rolled another stone and they did not jump as far. When he rolled the third stone they only looked around to see that it was just another stone. Then Coyote rolled himself up in a ball like Mountain Lion and rolled down the hill. When he got there he jumped up and tried to get a deer but he couldn't. He was too dizzy. He just fell over and the deer ran away.

The Sweetest Berry on the Bush

BY NUBIA KAI

Nubia Kai, a contemporary African-American fiction writer and poet, is author of *Solos* (Michigan State University Press, 1988).

Why the Spider Brings Money

Long, long ago in a small village in Ethiopia there lived a sheepherder and his wife and children—a boy and girl named Asman and Ama. Every morning Asman and Ama did their chores around the farm before watching the sheep in the pasture.

One afternoon, while tending the sheep, Asman spotted a big brown spider crawling along the bark of a tree. He raised his staff to kill it. Ama saw Asman and grabbed the staff.

"Don't, Asman! Don't kill that spider. Why you wanna kill a poor li'l spider that don't do nothing to you? That's so mean," said Ama.

"Get out of my way. Who are you to tell me what to do? You li'l flea. You give order to me, your big brother, eh?" Asman was four years older than his baby sister, and as was custom, he expected respect and obedience from her. Although Asman was older, Ama was wiser and more compassionate than her brother. When she challenged his authority, his pride was wounded, so he was even more determined to kill the spider.

"Get out of my way 'for I beat you."

"I won't. I won't let you kill that spider. Beat me all you want."

Asman hit her on the arm with his staff. Ama tore into her brother like a bull, knocking him to the ground. The staff fell from his hand. They rolled and tumbled in the grass, but Asman was much stronger than Ama. He put her across his legs and spanked her.

When they returned home early that evening, Asman told his parents that Ama had disobeyed him. Ama got another whipping from her parents for disobeying her older brother.

Not long after that, the sheep got sick with a contagious disease and started dying off in large numbers. Soon the family was in debt and so poor they could barely feed themselves. They had no choice but to leave and move to the big city of Napata to try to find food among the beggars of the city.

On their last night at the farm, a spider came to Ama's room. Ama recognized the spider in the moonlight.

"Ama!" The spider called her name. Ama jumped straight up on her bed of straw mats. "Don't be afraid, daughter of Anu. I've come to help, not to harm. You saved my life. You remember that day your brother tried to kill me, and you wouldn't let him? You fought him and took a whipping from him to save me. Bless your precious heart. You protected me like a mother protects her child. So because of your kindness, I have come back to protect you and your family in the same way. You are courageous and good, and the gods have spoken in your favor."

"I will place a pot of gold at your front door. When your father opens the door in the morning, he will discover it. He'll buy a thousand new sheep, and his farm will prosper like never before.

"And from now on, every time I appear to one of your descendants, I will be a sign of money, of wealth. And your people are not to kill me, but acknowledge that I am a messenger of the god of fortune. Give thanks and share what you have, and your life will increase in abundance." Having made his pronouncement, the spider tipped out of the window on its silent legs.

The next morning a pot of gold was sitting at the end of the porch. When the sheep farmer opened the door, he discovered the fortune. He knew it was from the gods and fell on his knees in praise of their generosity.

Just as the spider had predicted, he purchased a thousand sheep and a thousand more acres of land and became the most prosperous sheep farmer in the region.

And that is why we don't kill spiders, because of the kindness of Ama long, long ago in Ethiopia.

Chinese Fables

Chinese Fables, known as *yuyen,* are short stories featuring animal or human characters. Unlike other fable traditions, however, they tend not to make the lesson explicit in the form of a "moral." In recent years, though, some Chinese fabulists have played with a more Aesopic form, often "translating" them in transformative ways that address a Chinese appreciation of both narrative and lesson.

The Orangutans

The orangutans lived in compact communities deep in the mountains. Since they always moved about in groups of hundreds, hunters found it difficult to catch them. Then the hunters decided to offer enticements. The orangutans loved spirits, so the hunters put jars of spirits and distillers' grain by the road. The orangutans liked to wear clogs, so the hunters wove straw sandals in the style of clogs and put them by the roadside, connecting all of them with one rope.

Seeing the liquor and straw sandals by the road, the orangutans knew they were traps, so they cursed, "You fools! It's ridiculous to think you can seduce us with this stuff!"

Then they left, but returned a few minutes later. They did this several times, then said, "Let's just have a taste! There's no danger in just having a taste." But the more they tasted, the more delicious the spirits seemed, until they were all very drunk. They put on the straw sandals, but they could not walk, for all the shoes were bound together. In this way all of them fell into the trap.

Vegetarian Cat

The mouse always scampered at the sight of the cat, so the cat hit upon an idea. It hung a string of monk's beads around its neck. The mouse was very pleased at this, thinking to itself, "The cat has become a vegetarian. Isn't it wonderful?" To show thanks, a group of mice went to the cat. Seeing the mice had fallen into its trap, the cat uttered a loud cry and devoured a couple of mice one after the other. The rest fled pell-mell. Out of danger, the mice stuck out their tongues and said, "The cat is all the more ferocious since becoming vegetarian."

Yang Bu Beats His Dog

Once Yang Zhu's brother, Yang Bu, went out dressed in white. It rained, so he took off his white clothes and put on a black suit to go home. However, when he arrived home, his dog mistook him for a stranger and barked at him fiercely.

Greatly angered, Yang Bu grabbed a stick to beat it.

Yang Zhu stopped him, saying, "Don't beat it. Just put yourself in its place and you would do the same. Would you recognize your dog if it went out as a white dog and came back as a black one?"

The Owl Moves House

When it was moving house, the owl met a turtledove. The turtledove asked, "Where are you going in such a hurry?" "I'm moving to the east," answered the owl.

"Why?"

"Because," answered the owl, "people here are all complaining about my singing."

The turtledove said, "Moving to another place would be a good idea if you could change your voice. If you can't, the people in the east will complain about your voice as well."

Killing His Father by Hitting a Fly

A long time ago a man who hated flies always ran after them with a club.

Once when he saw some flies landing on his father's head, he became furious. He aimed at the flies and hit his father's head. His father's head was split open and the flies flew away.

He was sent to court by the neighbors and sentenced to death on a charge of murdering his own father.

It is not that he didn't love his father, but he hated flies so much he killed his own father.

A Hen and a Crow

At Tunze there was an old Sichuan hen that had colorful body feathers and red neck feathers. One day a group of chicks was following her on the threshing ground looking for food.

Suddenly an eagle flew over. Afraid that it might snatch her little chicks, the hen covered them with her big wings. After a little while the eagle flew away without catching anything.

A moment later a crow landed on the ground to look for food. Treating it like a brother, the old hen didn't think it would catch her chicks. Seeing that the hen was not watching, the crow took away one of her chicks.

Looking helplessly into the sky, the hen felt very sad and regretted having been fooled by the crow.

The Wolf and the Lamb
(Contemporary Chinese)

by Ying Wu

Ying Wu is a contemporary Chinese writer of fables, who combines wit and irony, the Aesopian with the Chinese tradition.

After having devoured a lamb, the wolf licked its lips and sighed, "Each time I catch a sheep, I have to find a new excuse. That's too difficult. I must think of another way."

Several days later, the wolf came across another lamb by a river. The wolf cried, "Hey! What are you doing here?"

The lamb replied, "I'm drinking water, sir."

The wolf said, "Drinking water? Don't you know you'll pollute the river? The animals and humans along the banks will suffer. When the water flows into the ocean, the animals and people of the whole world will suffer and die too. So, you see, you've brought disaster upon the universe!"

"Oh!" The lamb was struck dumb by this absurd accusation. After a long pause he said, "But I've been examined by the vet, who says I have no disease at all, sir."

"H'm!" Glaring fiendishly, the wolf continued, "You say you have no disease, but what about your parents? Do you think your grandparents, your grandparents-in-law and their parents were all healthy? And what value has this checkup by the vet? Can you guarantee that he's qualified, that his examination was thorough, that his microscope and fluoroscope functioned well? Perhaps he was bribed? Can you . . ."

"Then, I won't drink water from now on, sir!" the lamb said starting to flee.

"Stop!" cried the wolf springing on the lamb. "You say you won't drink water any more. Isn't it a crime to pollute the air? I must get rid of you today!"

"Spare me, sir," the lamb cried "If you eat me up, you'll get an infection and die too."

The wolf roared with laughter and concluded with this sentence, "My creed is: I would rather sacrifice myself to protect others!"

—False charges are much better than all excuses. They can kill the innocent and glorify the murderers as saints.

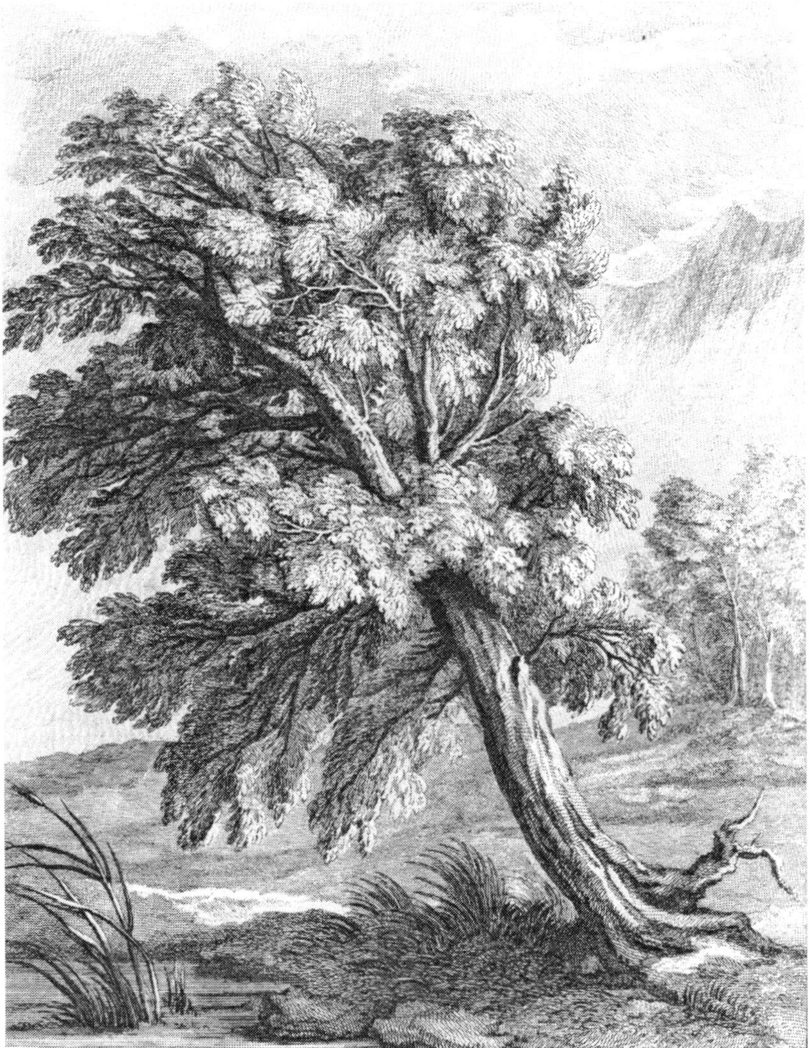

Fables

BY LEO TOLSTOY

Count Leo Tolstoy (1828-1910), the Russian writer famous for his novels *War and Peace* and *Anna Karenina*, also produced a series of fables that reflect his scornful attitude toward private property, his radical egalitarianism, and his rejection of church and state.

The Wolf and the Old Woman

A hungry wolf went hunting for food. In a hut at the edge of the village a little boy was crying, and the wolf overheard an old woman saying to him: "If you don't stop crying I'll give you to the wolf!" The wolf went no farther. He sat down and waited for the little boy to be given to him.

Night came and he was still waiting. Suddenly he heard the old woman say, "Don't cry, little one, I won't give you to the wolf. Just let that old wolf come, and we'll kill him!"

"There are evidently people here who say one thing and do another," thought the wolf. And he got up and left the village.

The Falcon and the Cock

The falcon was accustomed to his master and used to go and sit on his wrist when he was called, while the cock, when approached, ran away with a cry.

"You cocks are lacking in gratitude," said the falcon. "It is clear that you are a servile breed: you never go to your masters unless you are hungry. Not at all like us wild birds: we have great strength and can fly faster than any one, but we don't run from people—we go to them of our own free will when we are called. We don't forget that they feed us."

"You don't run from people," replied the cock, "because you have never seen roasted falcon, while we, from time to time, do see roasted chicken."

The Gnat and the Lion

A gnat flew up to a lion and said, "You think you're stronger than I am, don't you? Well, you are quite wrong! What sort of strength have you got? You scratch with your claws and gnaw with your teeth, the way peasant women fight with their husbands. I'm stronger than you are. Come on, let's fight!"

And sounding his trumpet, the gnat began to sting the lion on his bare nose and cheeks. The lion struck out with his paws, tearing and clawing his face till it bled and he was exhausted.

Trumpeting with joy, the gnat flew away. But it was not long before he became entangled in a spider's web, and the spider started sucking his blood.

"I overpowered the lion, strongest of beasts," thought the gnat, "and now I am destroyed by a miserable spider!"

The Hedgehog and the Hare

One day the hare met the hedgehog and he said, "You wouldn't be so bad, hedgehog, except that your legs are crooked, and you stumble."

The hedgehog grew angry and said, "What are you laughing at? My crooked legs can run faster than your straight ones. Just let me go home for a moment, and then you and I shall run a race!"

The hedgehog went home and said to his wife, "I had an argument with the hare and we're going to run a race."

The hedgehog's wife said, "You must be out of your mind! How can you run a race with the hare? His legs are nimble, while yours are crooked and slow!"

"His legs may be nimble," replied the hedgehog, "but my wits are nimble. You have only to do as I tell you. Now, let us go to the field."

They went to the plowed field where the hare was waiting. "You hide at this end of the furrow," said the hedgehog to his wife. "The hare and I will start from the other end. As soon as he begins to run I'll turn around and go back. When he reaches this end you come out and say: 'I've been waiting here a long time for you!' He can't tell one of us from the other, and he'll think you are me."

The hedgehog's wife hid in the furrow, and the hare and the hedgehog started their race from the other end.

As soon as the hare began to run, the hedgehog turned back and hid in the furrow. When the hare reached the other end, what did he see?—There sat the hedgehog's wife!

"I've been waiting for you a long time!" she said.

"What a miracle!" thought the hare, who could not tell her from her husband. "How could he have outrun me?"

"Come," he said aloud, "let's run again!"

"All right!"

The hare set off, and when he arrived at the other end, what did he see?—There sat the hedgehog!

"Well, brother," he said, "at last you're here! I've been waiting a long time!"

"What a miracle!" thought the hare. "No matter how fast I run, he always outruns me!"

"Come," he said, "let us run again, and this time you won't beat me!"

"All right!" said the hedgehog.

The hare hopped away as fast as he could, but again the hedgehog sat waiting at the end of the furrow.

And thus the hare continued hopping from one end of the furrow to the other until he was exhausted.

He finally gave up and said that henceforth he would never argue again.

An Aesop Fable

BY LEON TROTSKY

Leon Trotsky (1879–1940), Russian Bolshevik revolutionary and head of the Red Army under Nicolai Lenin, was later banished by Josef Stalin and eventually assassinated in Mexico. Citing the "peasant wisdom" to be gleaned from Krylov's fables, Trotsky would sometimes use the fable form to make a political lesson. The Comintern, or so-called Third International, referred to here derisively as "Manuilsky's Institute," was an international association formed in 1919 by the Bolshevik Party to coordinate communist movements worldwide under Moscow's rule.

An Aesop Fable

From What Next? Vital Question for the German Proletariat, 1932

A cattle dealer once drove some bulls to the slaughterhouse. When night came, the butcher came with his sharp knife.

"Let us close ranks and jack up this executioner on our horns," suggested one of the bulls.

"If you please, in what way is the butcher any worse than the dealer who drove us hither with his cudgel?" replied the bulls, who had received their political education in Manuilsky's institute.

"But we shall be able to attend to the dealer as well afterwards!"

"Nothing doing," replied the bulls firm in their principles, to the counselor. "You are trying, from the left, to shield our enemies—you are a social-butcher yourself."

And they refused to close ranks.

Peace Among the Beasts

BY COLETTE

Colette (1873–1954), a French writer mainly known for her saucy romances and intimate recollections, also wrote a good number of "animal stories" many of which clearly qualify as fables for their extraction of moral lessons from the narrative.

The Bear and the Old Lady

Spring 1914

Half past twelve is the hour for parliamentarians to lunch in a restaurant close to the Madeleine. At the table next to us, dine two men whose names I do not know, but it is not hard to predict that, after they have finished their cigars, their coffee and glass of brandy, they will cross the bridge to bury themselves, across the way, in the Chamber of Deputies. . . .

Smartly dressed, they're a bit uneasy, like folks who know no other rest than that of mealtimes; they lean on their elbows, lounge about on their seats, play with a dessert knife as if it were a letter opener, and exude an absolute indifference for everything happening around them. They talk politics, their voices lowered, with a prudent and jaded air—not that I don't catch the same words appearing a hundred times in print that week, a hundred times told and retold by every mouth: "The Viviani plan . . . approaches to Doumergue . . . Peytral . . . Ribot . . . Bourgeois. . . ." Their discussion heats up, and despite myself, I am able to pick up the drift of their conversation.

"Procedures for debates, you call that procedures for debate, that's a polite way to put it . . ."

"I'm trying . . ."

"They don't debate, my dear: they each issue an ultimatum, and with what airs! In all this, we see some surprising people, each more categorical than the other: this one does not admit, that one cannot tolerate; to question So-and-So is to offend him mortally. Thing makes threats, it's not very clear in whose name or about what: at the least objection, he howls and in the place of argumentation he substitutes a war dance and frenetic exhortation. Gadget expresses himself only with pronouncements, generally of the excommunicative kind. . . .

"The best part is that, were we to inform ourselves a little, we would discover that Gadget scarcely exists, that Thing has no political background whatsoever, that So-and-So's stock is nil and that his thunder is just the rattling of a tin sheet. . . . But, we don't inform ourselves, we tremble. It's the rule of the Peremptory."

Wearied, the two men stop talking for a moment, and I restrain an indiscreet urge to enter into their conversation, in order to tell them a most true story, which their last few words have just evoked—the story of the bear and the old Polish lady.

An old Polish lady lived in Austria—I'm talking about what it was like fifty years ago—in a forested estate, where wolves and bears could still be found in the old woods. A she-bear, slightly hurt, was taken captive there. The lady took her in, taking care of her and healing her until she became the tamest creature in the world, to the point of following her around like a dog and sleeping on the living room rug.

One day, the old lady was taking a forest path to one of her farmyards, when she noticed that Macha, her pet she-bear, was following her.

"No, Macha," she told her, "you're not coming along, go back home."

Macha refused, got a bit stubborn, and so the Polish lady had to lead her back home herself, shutting her up safely in the living room.

Back in the forest, she once again hears a muffled trot on pine needles; she turns around and who does she see come running but . . . Macha, Macha who quickly catches up with her and stops right before her.

"Oh! Macha!" cried the old lady, "I told you not to follow me! I'm really cross with you now! I command you to go back home! Come on, get going!"

And she punctuates her speech—blam! blam!—with two little blows of her umbrella on Macha's nose. Macha looks at her mistress with an unsure eye, leaps aside and disappears into the brush . . .

"I made a mistake," thought the old lady. "Macha will no longer want to return home at all, she's upset. She'll terrorize the sheep and the cattle . . . I'm going to go back home and look for Macha."

She retraced her path, opened her living room door and found . . . Macha, Macha who had not gone anywhere, an irreproachable Macha dozing away on the rug! The beast in the woods was quite simply another bear, who was running up to eat the old lady, but upon being greeted by two little umbrella blows and scolded like a mere poodle, the bear said to itself:

"This authoritative person surely wields a mysterious and limitless power . . . better take off!"

But, anyway, what if the other bear, the wild one, had known that the lady, that peremptory old lady, was armed with nothing more than a little pink cotton umbrella . . . what then?

—*Translated by Georges Van Den Abbeele*

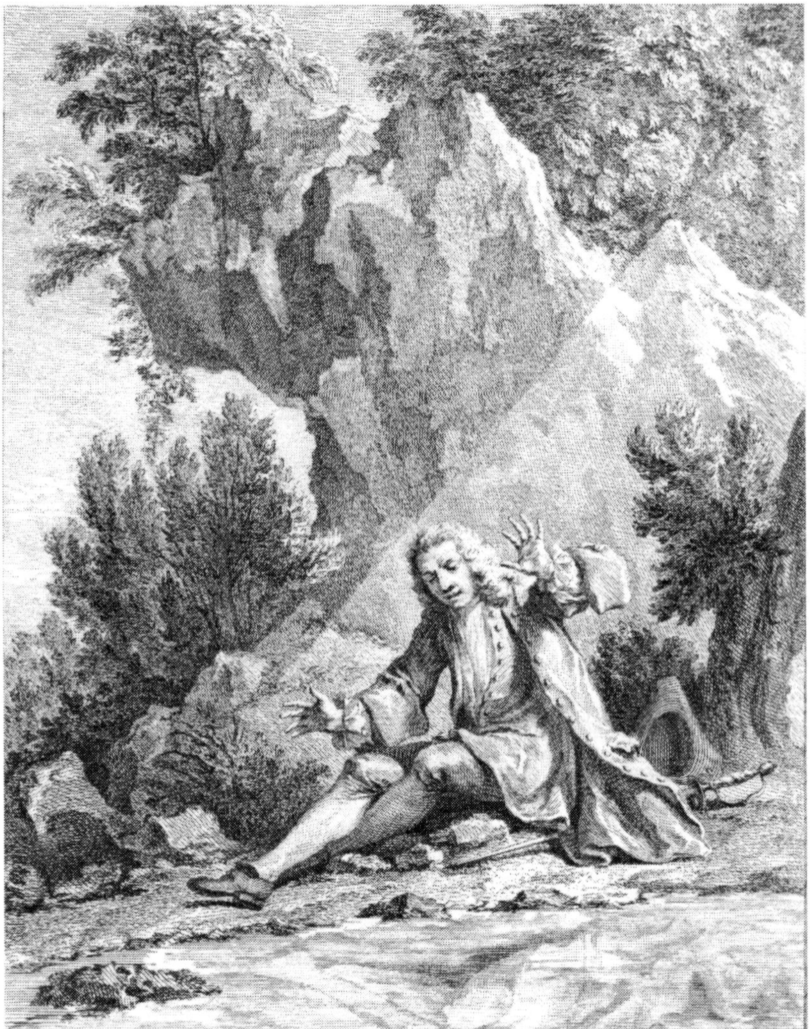

Fables for Our Time

BY JAMES THURBER

James Thurber, the noted American cartoonist and writer (1894–1961), graced the pages of *The New Yorker* during the mid-20th century with his urbane wit and humor. *Fables for Our Time* (1940) and *Further Fables for Our Time* (1956) offer a disabused overturning of the classic moralizing fable by more cynical lessons set in the reality of modern times.

The Elephant Who Challenged the World

Elephant who lived in Africa woke up one morning with the conviction that he could defeat all the other animals in the world in single combat, one at a time. He wondered that he hadn't thought of it before. After breakfast he called first on the lion. "You are only the King of Beasts," bellowed the elephant, "whereas I am the Ace!" and he demonstrated his prowess by knocking the lion out in fifteen minutes, no holds barred. Then in quick succession he took on the wild boar, the water buffalo, the rhinoceros, the hippopotamus, the giraffe, the zebra, the eagle, and the vulture, and he conquered them all. After that the elephant spent most of his time in bed eating peanuts, while the other animals, who were now his slaves, built for him the largest house any animal in the world had ever had. It was five stories high, solidly made of the hardest woods to be found in Africa. When it was finished, the Ace of Beasts moved in and announced that he could pin back the ears of any animal in the world. He challenged all comers to meet him in the basement of the big house, where he had set up a prize ring ten times the regulation size.

Several days went by and then the elephant got an anonymous letter accepting his challenge. "Be in your basement tomorrow afternoon at three o'clock," the message read. So at three o'clock the next day the elephant went down to the basement to meet his mysterious opponent, but there was no one there, or at least no one he could see. "Come out from behind whatever you're behind!" roared the elephant. "I'm not behind anything," said a tiny voice. The elephant tore around the basement, upsetting barrels and boxes, banging his head against the furnace pipes, rocking the house on its foundations, but he could not find his opponent. At the end of an hour the elephant roared that the whole business was a trick and a deceit—probably ventriloquism—and that he would never come down to the basement again.

"Oh, yes you will," said the tiny voice. "You will be down here at three o'clock tomorrow and you'll end up on your back." The elephant's laughter shook the house. "We'll see about that," he said.

The next afternoon the elephant, who slept on the fifth floor of the house, woke up at two-thirty and looked at his wristwatch. "Nobody I can't see will ever get me down to the basement again," he growled, and went back to sleep. At exactly three o'clock the house began to tremble and quiver as if an earthquake had it in its paws. Pillars and beams bent and broke like reeds, for they were all drilled full of tiny holes. The fifth floor gave way completely and crashed down upon the fourth, which fell upon the third, which fell upon the second, which carried away the first as if it had been the floor of a berry basket. The elephant was precipitated into the basement, where he fell heavily upon the concrete floor and lay there on his back, completely unconscious. A tiny voice began to count him out. At the count of ten the elephant came to, but he could not get up. "What animal are you?" he demanded of the mysterious voice in a quavering tone that had lost its menace.

"I am the termite," answered the voice.

The other animals, straining and struggling for a week, finally got the elephant lifted out of the basement and put him in jail. He spent the rest of his life there, broken in spirit and back.

Moral: The battle is sometimes to the small, for the bigger they are the harder they fall.

Further Fables for Our Time
"Variations on a Theme"

I

A fox, attracted by the scent of something, followed his nose to a tree in which sat a crow with a piece of cheese in his beak. "Oh, cheese," said the fox scornfully. "That's for mice."

The crow removed the cheese with his talons and said, "You always hate the thing you cannot have, as, for instance, grapes."

"Grapes are for the birds," said the fox haughtily. "I am an epicure, a gourmet, and a gastronome."

The embarrassed crow, ashamed to be seen eating mouse food by a great specialist in the art of dining, hastily dropped the cheese. The fox caught it deftly, swallowed it with relish, said "*Merci*," politely, and trotted away.

II

A fox had used all his blandishments in vain, for he could not flatter the crow in the tree and make him drop the cheese he held in his beak. Suddenly, the crow tossed the cheese to the astonished fox. Just then the farmer, from whose kitchen the loot had been stolen, appeared, carrying a rifle, looking for the robber. The fox turned and ran for the woods. "There goes the guilty son of a vixen now!" cried the crow, who, in case you do not happen to know it can see the glint of sunlight on a gun barrel at a greater distance than anybody.

III

This time the fox, who was determined not to be outfoxed by a crow, stood his ground and did not run when the farmer appeared, carrying a rifle and looking for the robber.

"The teeth marks in this cheese are mine," said the fox, "but the beak marks were made by the true culprit up there in the tree. I submit this cheese in evidence, as Exhibit A, and bid you and the criminal a very good day." Whereupon he lit a cigarette and strolled away.

IV

In the great and ancient tradition, the crow in the tree with the cheese in his beak began singing, and the cheese fell into the fox's lap. "You sing like a shovel," said the fox, with a grin, but the crow pretended not to hear and cried out, "Quick, give me back the cheese! Here comes the farmer with his rifle!"

"Why should I give you back the cheese?" the wily fox demanded.

"Because the farmer has a gun, and I can fly faster than you can run."

So the frightened fox tossed the cheese back to the crow, who ate it, and said, "Dearie me, my eyes are playing tricks on me—or am I playing tricks on you? Which do you think?" But there was no reply, for the fox had slunk away into the woods.

Italian Folk Tales

BY ITALO CALVINO

Italo Calvino (1923–1984) was born in Cuba of Italian parents and lived most of his life in Italy. Author of *The Nonexistent Knight*, *The Cloven Viscount*, and *Italian Folk Tales*, among other works, he is considered one of the great Italian writers of the 20th century.

The Wolf and the Three Girls

Once there were three sisters who worked in a certain town. Word reached them one day that their mother, who lived in Borgoforte, was deathly ill. The oldest sister therefore filled two baskets with four bottles of wine and four cakes and set out for Borgoforte. Along the way she met the wolf, who said to her, "Where are you going in such haste?"

"To Borgoforte to see Mama, who is gravely ill."

"What's in those baskets?"

"Four bottles of wine and four cakes."

"Give them to me, or else—to put it bluntly—I'll eat you."

The girl gave the wolf everything and went flying back home to her sisters. Then the middle girl filled her baskets and left for Borgoforte. She too met the wolf.

"Where are you going in such haste?"

"To Borgoforte to see Mama, who is gravely ill."

"What's in those baskets?"

"Four bottles of wine and four cakes."

"Give them to me, or else—to put it bluntly—I'll eat you."

So the second sister emptied her baskets and ran home. Then the youngest girl said, "Now it's my turn." She prepared the baskets and set out. There was the wolf.

"Where are you going in such haste?"

"To Borgoforte to see Mama, who is gravely ill."

"What's in those baskets?"

"Four bottles of wine and four cakes."

"Give them to me, or else—to put it bluntly—I'll eat you."

The little girl took a cake and threw it to the wolf, who had his mouth open. She had made the cake especially for him and filled it with nails. The wolf caught it and bit into it, pricking his palate all over. He spat out the cake, leaped back, and ran off shouting, "You'll pay for that!"

Taking certain short cuts known only to him, the wolf ran ahead and reached Borgoforte before the little girl. He slipped into the sick mother's house, gobbled her up, and took her place in bed.

The little girl arrived, found her mother with the sheet drawn up to her eyes, and said, "How dark you've become, Mama!"

"That's because I've been sick so much, my child," said the wolf.

"How big your head has become, Mama!"

"That's because I've worried so much, my child."

"Let me hug you, Mama," said the little girl, and the wolf gobbled her up whole.

With the little girl in his belly, the wolf ran out of the house. But the townspeople, seeing him come out, chased him with pitchforks and shovels, cornered him, and killed him. They slit him open at once and out came mother and daughter still alive. The mother got well, and the girl went back and said to her sisters, "Here I am, safe and sound!"

Uncle Wolf

There was once a greedy little girl. One day during carnival time, the schoolmistress said to the children, "If you are good and finish your knitting, I will give you pancakes."

But the little girl didn't know how to knit and asked for permission to go to the privy. There she sat down and fell asleep. When she came back into school, the other children had eaten all the pancakes. She went home crying and told her mother what had happened.

"Be a good little girl, my poor dear," said her mother. "I'll make pancakes for you." But her mother was so poor she didn't even have a skillet. "Go to Uncle Wolf and ask him if he'll lend us his skillet."

The little girl went to Uncle Wolf's house and knocked. Knock, knock.

"Who is it?"

"It's me!"

"For years and months, no one has knocked at this door! What do you want?"

"Mama sent me to ask if you'll lend us your skillet to make pancakes."

"Just a minute, let me put my shirt on."

Knock, knock.

"Just a minute, let me put on my drawers."

Knock, knock.

"Just a minute, let me put on my pants."

Knock, knock.

"Just a minute, let me put on my overcoat."

Finally Uncle Wolf opened the door and gave her the skillet. "I'll lend it to you, but tell Mama to return it full of pancakes, together with a round loaf of bread and a bottle of wine."

"Yes, yes, I'll bring you everything."

When she got home, her mother made her a whole stack of pancakes, and also a stack for Uncle Wolf. Before nightfall she said to the child, "Take the pancakes to Uncle Wolf together with this loaf of bread and bottle of wine."

Along the way the child, glutton that she was, began sniffing the pancakes. "Oh, what a wonderful smell! I think I'll try just one." But then she had to eat another and another and another, and soon the pancakes were all gone and followed by the bread, down to the last crumb, and the wine, down to the last drop.

Now to fill up the skillet she raked up some donkey manure from off the road. She refilled the bottle with dirty water. To replace the bread, she made a round loaf out of the lime she got from a stonemason working along the way. When she reached Uncle Wolf's, she gave him this ugly mess.

Uncle Wolf bit into a pancake. "Uck! This is donkey dung!" He uncorked the wine at once to wash the bad taste out of his mouth. "Uck! This is dirty water!" He bit off a piece of bread. "Uck! This is lime!" He glared at the child and said, "Tonight I'm coming to eat you!"

The child ran home to her mother. "Tonight Uncle Wolf is coming to eat me!"

Her mother went around closing doors and windows and stopping up all the holes in the house, so Uncle Wolf couldn't get in; but she forgot to stop up the chimney.

When it was night and the child was already in bed, Uncle Wolf's voice was heard outside the house. "I'm going to eat you now. I'm right outside!" Then a footstep was heard on the roof. "I'm going to eat you now! I'm on the roof!"

Then a clatter was heard in the chimney. "I'm going to eat you now. I'm in the chimney!"

"Mama, Mama! The wolf is here!"

"Hide under the covers!"

"I'm going to eat you now. I'm on the hearth!"

Shaking like a leaf, the child curled up as small as possible in a corner of the bed.

"I'm going to eat you now I'm in the room!"

The little girl held her breath.

"I'm going to eat you now! I'm at the foot of the bed! Ahem, here I go!" And he gobbled her up.

So Uncle Wolf always eats greedy little girls.

Contemporary Italian

BY CARLA MUSCHIO

Carla Muschio (born 1955) is a contemporary Milanese Italian writer who has translated Lewis Carroll, Leo Tolstoy, and Mark Twain into Italian. In addition, she has produced a number of fables and stories for children.

Where Do Children Come From?

Above the clouds, in the sky, there is a magnificent garden with blooming plants of all hues and scents. It is God's garden. All the animals of the world live there in freedom. If they look down from the borders of the garden they can see the earth.

A little lion liked to look to earth from a balustrade not far from his den. One day he looked down and he saw something that he had never known. Not only were there lands, seas, rivers, and mountains; not only were there plants and flowers similar to those in heaven, not only were there the same animals as in his garden, some new beings had appeared. The little lion called his mother asking for an explanation, but she didn't know those animals either. The little lion was not shy: he went to God's house and asked. And God explained.

"Those are men and women of the earth. They are my last creation. Do you like them?"

"I do," said the little lion. "And what do the cubs of humans look like?"

"I don't know, I haven't thought of cubs yet."

So the little lion, who was adventurous, had an idea. He asked with just a slight hesitation in his voice.

"Could I become a cub of humans?"

God looked at him for a while without answering. God was thinking. Finally God said.

"Why not, but then you must change something in your character. As a lion you are fine the way you are, but with your idea of justice you cannot be a child of humans. Among humans nobody must take the lion's share. Rights and justice must be the same for everyone. What do you think of this?"

"What do you mean, the same for everyone? Would you say that a little frog or a dragonfly is equal to me, the king of the forest?"

"If you want to become a child, you must accept having exactly the same rights as everybody else—no less—no more. Even if you were to become a king of men, you wouldn't be worth more than anybody else. Do you accept that?"

The little lion was so curious about going down to earth that he accepted. He promised he would become just.

No sooner said than done, God turned him into a beautiful, strong boy. One of God's servants took him in his arms and delivered him to earth.

Neither God nor the little lion was aware that they were not alone. A little pig who was rolling in the mud close by, behind a bush, had heard everything. He ran and looked down from the balustrade of the sky and he saw a woman of the earth happily lulling the little lion, now her baby. The little pig wanted to do the same, and, without a moment's hesitation, without even wiping the mud from his body, he went to find God.

God had fallen asleep and was dreaming of new universes, but the great noise that the little pig made startled God.

The rash little pig spoke up.

"I have seen that on earth there are some new animals."

God said their name, "Humans."

"And also small ones," said the little pig. God nodded and said their name.

"Children."

"And how about that child? Did he use to be my friend, the little lion?"

Once again God nodded.

"If that is so," declared the little pig, "I also want to become a child of the earth."

But God objected, "Do you know how I want the children of the earth to be? All healthy and clean. They all must have, beside good food, fresh water to wash themselves and to drink. And you, such a lover of mud, how will you manage?"

"If they really feed me well, I promise that I shall always wash myself."

"They will surely feed you well. All the children of the earth must be able to eat and drink and grow with good health. So, do you really want to become a child?"

The little pig nodded his head. God called a servant, who flew down to earth and laid a chubby baby into a cot. And a happy woman took into her arms the child fallen from heaven.

On that day in the garden in the sky there was a lot of speaking of the great novelties: the people of the earth, the little pig and the lion who had become children.

A pretty little elephant became curious. She went dancing on the grass looking for God. God was presiding at court. Although God was eating, God let the little elephant in all the same and asked her what she wanted.

"On the earth there are no baby girls as yet. I would like to be the first one."

"This is really a good idea," God answered. "Because, do you know how I want the children of the earth to be? As beloved, pretty and cuddling as you are. They must all have a mother and a father and grow up happy and well looked after. Exactly the way you are growing, little elephant."

"So, may I also go down on the earth?"

The little elephant almost couldn't believe it, but God had her be immediately carried down to earth, among people. She was the prettiest little girl one could imagine. Her mother put a bracelet on her arm and showed her to everybody, so beautiful she was.

Days passed. In the sky there lived a little donkey that was not very intelligent, but he was good-hearted and gentle. While looking down on the earth, he saw some children happily playing.

A fox came by. The little donkey questioned her.

"Who are those cubs?"

"Oh, my dear donkey, they were once animals in our garden, but now they are children, the small ones of humans. If you ask God, perhaps you too can go to the earth. The little donkey could not understand how it could have happened, since he was not very clever, but he was curious. So he went looking for God. God was always kind. On seeing the little donkey God immediately asked him what he wanted.

And the donkey answered directly, "I also want to go down to the earth and be a child."

God laughed, and then said: "My dear little donkey, I like to grant wishes, but this one is really impossible. The children of the earth must rank among my best creations. And so I want them to be learned and intelligent. They must all be able to study, they must all be able to read and write and count. And not only that, but also to think and to invent. And how could you do all this, my dear little donkey?"

"What if I promise to do my best?"

God started to think while the little donkey was trustfully waiting. After thinking for a long time, God came up with an idea.

"All right little donkey, I want to grant your desire. If you really want to, you will become a child of humans. But on the earth there will be places called schools where all the children will have to go to study so as to become learned and wise. Do you promise to go to school?"

So great was his desire to try this new adventure that the little donkey accepted.

This was a long time ago. The world is full of children who once were pigs, elephants, lions, donkeys and also other animals, who wanted to go down and live on earth. This is why some children are as mischievous as monkeys, as stubborn as mules, as rash as lions, or as dirty as pigs. If they aren't careful, they go back to the habits they had before, when they were living in the sky. But God, who is often indulgent, is inflexible on one thing: God wants all children to be well-cared-for and most of all happy.

Hottentot Fables

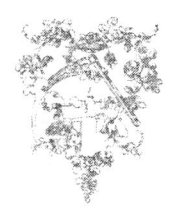

The tales were collected in the middle of the 19th century and as such represent an insight into the authentic oral tradition of the Hottentot people of South Africa. The group tells stories about jackals, lions, tortoises, leopards, and elephants.

The Tortoises Hunting the Ostriches

One day, it is said, the Tortoises held a council how they might hunt Ostriches, and they said, "Let us, on both sides, stand in rows near each other, and let one go to hunt the Ostriches, so that they must flee along through the midst of us." They did so, and as they were so many, the Ostriches were obliged to run along through the midst of the Tortoises. During this they did not move, but, remaining always in the same places, called each to the other, "Are you there?" and each one answered, "I am here." The Ostriches hearing this, ran so tremendously that they quite exhausted their strength, and fell down. Then the Tortoises assembled by-and-by at the place where the Ostriches had fallen, and devoured them.

The Giraffe and the Tortoise

The Giraffe and the Tortoise, they say, met one day. The Giraffe said to the Tortoise, "At once I could trample you to death." The Tortoise, being afraid, remained silent. Then the Giraffe said, "At once I could swallow you." The Tortoise said, in answer to this, "Well, I just belong to the family of those whom it has always been customary to swallow." Then the Giraffe swallowed the Tortoise; but when the latter was being gulped down, it stuck in the Giraffe's throat, and as the Giraffe could not get it down, he was choked to death.

When the Giraffe was dead, the Tortoise crawled out and went to the Crab (who is considered the mother of the Tortoise), and told her what had happened. Then the Crab said, "The little Crab! I could sprinkle it under its arm with boochoo [a token of approval according to Hottentot custom].

The crooked-legged little one, I could sprinkle under its arm."

The Tortoise answered its mother and said—

"Have you not always sprinkled me,
That you want to sprinkle me now?"

Then they went and fed for a whole year on the remains of the Giraffe.

Which Was the Thief?

A Jackal and a Hyena went and hired themselves to a man to be his servants. In the middle of the night the Jackal rose and smeared the Hyena's tail with some fat, and then ate all the rest of the fat in the house. In the morning the man missed his fat, and he immediately accused the Jackal of having eaten it.

"Look at the Hyena's tail," said the rogue, "and you will see who is the thief." The man did so, and then thrashed the Hyena till she was nearly dead.

The Lion and the Baboon

The Baboon, it is said, once worked bamboos, sitting on the edge of a precipice, and the Lion stole upon him. The Baboon, however, had fixed some round, glistening, eye-like plates on the back of his head. When, therefore, the Lion crept upon him, he thought, when the Baboon was looking at him, that he sat with his back towards him, and crept with all his might upon him. When, however, the Baboon turned his back towards him, the Lion thought that he was seen, and hid himself. Thus, when the Baboon looked at him, he crept upon him. Whilst the Baboon did this, the Lion came close upon him. When he was near him the Baboon looked up, and the Lion continued to creep up on him. The Baboon said (aside), "Whilst I am looking at him he steals upon me, whilst my hollow eyes are on him."

When at last the Lion sprung at him, he lay (quickly) down upon his face, and the Lion jumped over him, falling down the precipice, and was dashed to pieces.

Ananse Stories From Ghana

The main character of most of the Ghanaian fables is the spider. He is tricky, clever, and appears in almost any location. In Nigeria, the main character of the fable is usually a tortoise, whereas in Kenya, the Kikuyu fables feature a rabbit.

How the Spider Paid His Debts

One day the spider realized that he had contracted a great number of debts. In fact, he had borrowed from every animal in the forest, and he took counsel with himself as to what he should do, for he had no money with which to pay. Then he sent word to all his creditors to meet him on a certain Friday so that he could pay them.

When the Friday came, and while it was still early in the morning, the hen arrived to collect her debt. And when she came, the spider said, "Good, I will pay at once; but wait a minute or two while I prepare you some food." So the hen waited inside the hut while the spider went outside. Soon the cat came. The spider said to him, "Good. The repayment is in the hut," and so the cat went and entered the hut and seized the hen and twisted her neck. Just as the cat was about to go away, the dog arrived, and the spider said, "Good. The repayment is in the hut; go and take it." So the dog went and seized the cat and killed him. Just as the dog was about to go, the hyena arrived; and the spider said, "Good. The repayment is in the hut; go and take it. So the hyena ran in and seized the dog and ate him. Just as the hyena was about to leave, the leopard appeared; and the spider said, "Good. The repayment is in the hut; go and take it." So the leopard sprang upon the hyena and killed him. Just as the leopard was about to leave the lion arrived; and when he saw his enemy the leopard, they began to fight. While they were fighting the spider took some pepper and sprinkled it in their eyes. After that he took up a big stick and beat them until they were both dead. Then the spider and his family collected the meat and had a great feast.

The Spider and the Fox

Once upon a time the spider challenged the fox to a race. Before the day appointed for the contest, the spider entered into league with all his companions and arranged that they should station themselves at regular intervals along the course and that each should wait in readiness to answer the calls of the fox as he raced along the course to the finish line. As soon as the race started, the fox began outstripping the spider with ease, and he called back in mocking tones to ask where the spider was. To his surprise the answer, "Here I am" came from the opposite direction to what he expected. He raced along once more, and repeated the challenge. Again a voice answered from in front of him, and once more he was deceived into thinking that he was being left behind in the race. The strategy was repeated all along the course, until the fox fell exhausted and could not finish. The spider then dashed forward and won the race. This made the fox so angry, when he revived, that he vowed to get even with the spider. And to this very day he has been looking for the spider; but the spider hides himself in the corners of houses out of the path of the fox, because he knows what is in store for him if ever the fox should confront him.

Ogoni Folk Tales

BY KEN SARO-WIWA

Ken Saro-Wiwa (1941–1995), an Ogoni Nigerian, was executed in 1995 by the Nigerian government because of his political actions on behalf of the Ogoni people, an ethnic group of 500,000 who live near Port Harcourt, Nigeria, the site of one of the largest oil reserves in Nigeria. Saro-Wiwa was the target of government persecution because of his leadership in protests against environmentally destructive oil drilling in his Ogoni homeland. The main character of most of the stories is Kuru, the Tortoise, a creature whose cunning and wisdom help him survive.

Crime and Punishment

Once upon a time, and a time it was indeed, Kuru the Tortoise and Lion were very good friends. They had grown up together and had each a wife and children. Lion's wife was very pretty. Even after she had had five children, she still looked youthful and her breasts were firm. Everyone admired her. Kuru, her husband's best friend, desired her secretly. He longed for the day he could make love to her. He was on his farm, one day, when opportunity came knocking at his door.

"Good morning, Ter Kuru," respectfully greeted Mrs. Lion as she walked past the farm, a pot on her head. She was on her way to the stream to fetch water.

"Good morning, beautiful wife of my dear friend," replied Kuru cheerfully. "Please stop by on your way back. I have to give you something for my friend, your dear husband."

"I will," answered Mrs. Lion.

While she was gone, Kuru quickly made fire, roasted a yam, brushed it clean, sliced it, and put a sedative juice on the slices. Then he waited.

Dutifully and without suspicion, Mrs. Lion stopped at Kuru's farm on her return from the stream. Kuru welcomed her warmly and helped her place her water pot on the ground.

"Would you like to have some yam with me?" asked Kuru.

"I'm about to have my breakfast!"

"I'm sorry I cannot. I'm in a hurry. What is it you wanted to send to my husband?" asked Mrs. Lion.

"What's the hurry? Come on, have a bite of breakfast."

Mrs. Lion reluctantly agreed to eat the yam that Kuru offered her.

It was tasty. As soon as she finished eating, she felt drowsy and slept off. Kuru had got his long-awaited opportunity. While she slept, he made love to her. When Mrs. Lion woke up, she realized what had happened and wept profusely. Kuru pleaded with her to stop weeping, but she had been defiled and was inconsolable.

"I'll give you whatever you ask for," pleaded Kuru. "Please stop crying and don't let your husband know."

Mrs. Lion left her pot at Kuru's farm and cried all the way home. When she got there, she, sobbing, told her husband how Kuru the Tortoise had deceived her.

Lion was highly infuriated. He growled and roared. He did not believe that anyone would dare him in such a manner. He who was king of all the animals! He refused to believe that his best friend, Kuru, would betray him—with his wife. He decided to ask his friend whether what he had heard was true.

"I'm sorry," pleaded Kuru. "It was the work of the devil. In fact, I didn't know what I was doing until it was all over. Please forgive me. I will pay you whatever you demand in recompense. I know I have wronged you." This confession only enraged Lion the more. He growled and roared, bundled Kuru away and tied him to a stake in front of his house.

Kuru remained tied to the stake under sun and rain for months. Secretly, at night, his wife would bring him food. She and her family pleaded daily with Lion to release Kuru. But Lion was adamant. Antelope, Tiger, Elephant and other animals were sent as emissaries to him but he turned them away contemptuously. Meanwhile, Kuru suffered. His skin began to peel off and he felt sickly.

People began to feel sorry for Kuru. Nobody, they said, was a saint. We all commit offenses from time to time. And was not Lion himself notorious for his outrageous crimes?

He did not own farmland. All he did was feed on other animals. Indeed, if he had killed and eaten Kuru, his best friend, no one would have been surprised. But they could not challenge Lion to his face. They were afraid of what he might do to them. They only pleaded with him. But the more they pleaded, the more Lion remained strong in his resolve to punish Kuru. He wanted to kill Kuru slowly.

One day, Rabbit was on his way to the farm and saw Kuru in his pitiable condition. "Kuru, are you still there?" asked Rabbit. "Is it not over twelve months since all this began?"

"What can I do?" replied Kuru. "Some people want to clear the world of sin. But do not worry about me. I already know my fate. I wish my friend would kill me right away."

"Your friend adds insult to injury! He's a wanderer and a thief. And did he not threaten Monkey's wife the other day beside the stream after sleeping with her? The poor lady was too frightened to tell anyone, but I saw him myself. And whose wife has been safe from his amorous advances? Whose wife?"

News of Kuru's plight soon passed from ear to ear until Lion himself heard it. Although he was not unduly perturbed, it reminded him that Kuru was still his prisoner. His anger had worn off, but he had promised not to release Kuru himself. He wished the miserable adulterer would die. His presence in front of his house did not please him.

Thus, when Kuru pleaded again with him, saying, "If you won't kill me right away, send me to the forest where I can die in peace," Lion quickly agreed. He took Kuru to a secret part of the forest and dumped him there, hoping that no one would find him.

Kuru remained in the forest for days, unbeknown to all. It began to be noised abroad that Lion had murdered Kuru.

Kuru's family wept bitterly. And everyone was angry with Lion and began to look upon him as a criminal. Kuru's offense, they agreed, was minor.

So it was that when a hunter stumbled upon Kuru in the forest and brought him back home to his family, there was general rejoicing throughout the land. He was given a hero's welcome and songs were composed and sung in his honor. It is advisable to match punishment with offense lest we make a hero of an offender.

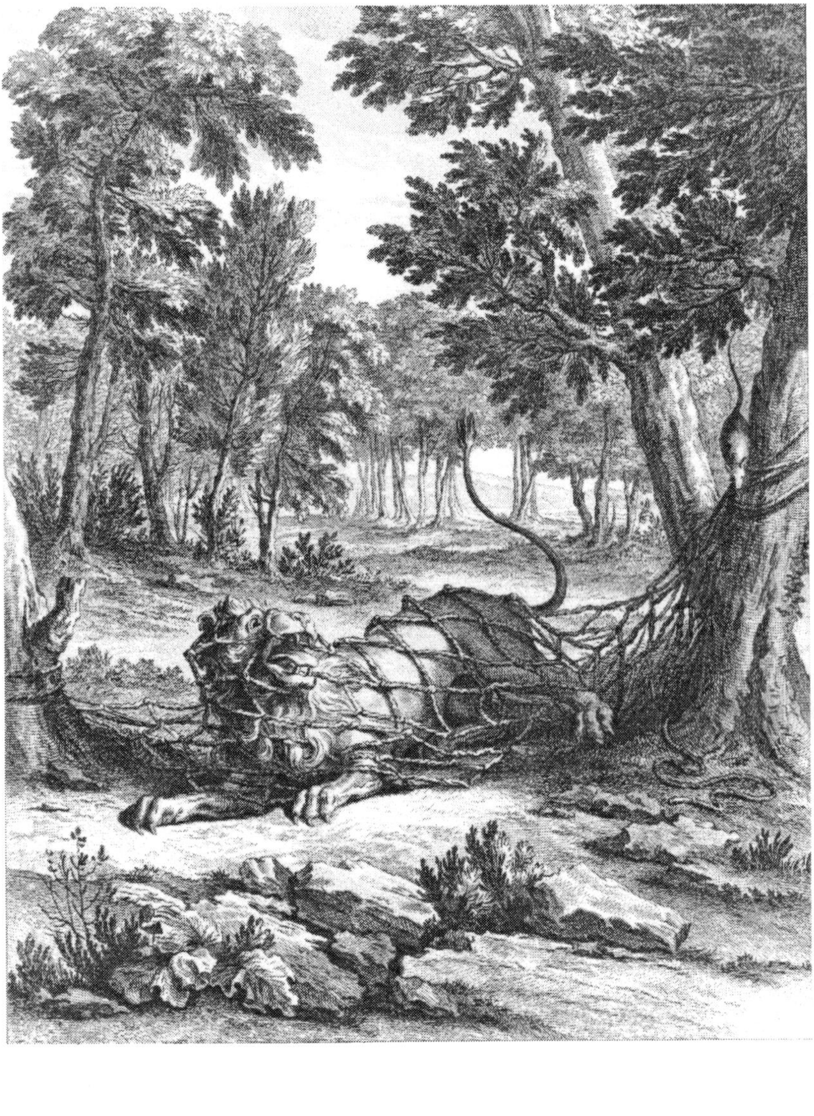

The Promise

Once upon a time, Kuru the Tortoise and Kue the Leopard were very good friends. A great drought had fallen upon the land and there was little food to eat. Kue had a great appetite and he and his family were almost dying of hunger.

One day, Kue paid his friend a visit. "Friend of friends," said he as soon as he had been made welcome, "how do you get by in these lean times?"

"Well, we do manage to live from day to day. Our requirements are moderate, as you well know!"

"I'm dying of hunger. My family too. Something will have to be done if I'm not to die!"

"What's to be done?" demanded Kuru.

"I have a plan," replied Kue. "Let's go hunting."

"But you know as well as I do that I'm not a good hunter."

"That's all right. Just accompany me. I'll do the hunting while you guard whatever we succeed in hunting."

"Accompany you? What if you should turn on me in your hunger and eat me up?"

"Friend of friends," replied Kue, "you know I'll do nothing of the sort. How could I be so unfair to my bosom friend? I need your services if my plan is to succeed. And we'll share the fruit of the hunt equally!"

"Are you sure?"

"Upon my word. Just keep your wits about you during the hunt. I will not turn on you, I promise."

"And if you do?"

"May the heavens kiss the earth and darkness bury all," swore Kue.

"Good. Now, tell me how we'll set about the hunt!"

"We'll have to go out in a canoe. You'll lay me at the prow thereof and I'll bare my teeth in a grin of death. The idea would be that I died of hunger. That should please a lot of animals. I bet some of them will want to throw an insult or two at me. Whoever does so will meet instant death. No one will blame me for killing an animal that dared insult me."

"That sounds quite sensible to me," Kuru said.

"Quite simple too. You don't have to do more than paddle the canoe and say one or two witty things when we meet a likely victim. I permit you to insult me as much as you like. I won't take offense!"

"Good. I'll come with you," Kuru replied finally. "But no tricks this time, I beg of you."

"It's a gentleman's agreement. We'll live like kings after the hunt."

They parted, that day, with a handshake and set a day for the hunt.

On the appointed day, they left at dawn for the river. Kue's canoe was moored to the riverbank. Kuru sat at the bow of the canoe, his face set in mourning. He used a mixture of saliva and seawater to give the impression that he was weeping tears of sorrow. Kue lay stretched out at the prow of the canoe, his teeth shining in an open mouth, his eyes shut. He looked ugly. Kuru untied the canoe and they moved out into the river. Kuru paddled on, keeping close to the trees on the bank of the river. He wept loudly to attract the attention of all animals.

The first animal they met was an antelope who had gone early that morning to fetch water. When she heard Kuru weeping loudly, her curiosity was aroused. She drew nearer the waterfront.

"Kuru, my brother," she called, "what's the matter?"

"Well, it's my friend, Kue, the Leopard!"

"What happened to him? Is he ill?"

"Oh, it's worse than that," sobbed Kuru sorrowfully. "He's dead."

"Dead? What of?"

"Dare you ask? It's the famine. You know Kue and his huge appetite. He couldn't stand the hunger one day longer. He came to beg me for food and collapsed on my doorstep."

"Serves him right!" replied the antelope. "The brute has been terrorizing my entire family these many years gone. Now we can live in peace. I should like to see him die many times over."

"That pleasure is yours for the mere asking, my dear," replied Kuru.

"How d'you mean?" asked the antelope.

"It's easy. Why don't you draw nearer and give the terrorist a few punches on the nose? It should serve him right and give you some satisfaction, eh?"

"To be sure, to be sure," replied the antelope.

And she clambered into the canoe to punch Kue on the nose. As she raised her right arm, up jumped Kue and pounced on the unfortunate antelope. In another moment, she lay at the bottom of the canoe, dead.

"That's one," said Kue with satisfaction.

"And a good one, if you ask me," replied Kuru gleefully. As Kue resumed his position at the prow of the canoe, Kuru paddled on and wept ever more loudly. Soon, they came across a rabbit.

"Ah, my friend, what's up?" asked the rabbit.

"It's Kue, the Leopard," Kuru answered.

"You've been able to lay the rogue low, eh?"

"Oh, yes. He had it coming a long time."

"Aren't you a great one, Kuru? I say, who else but you could have performed such a feat? Kue has been the terror of the place since creation. You'd have thought he'd never die."

"But there he lies. As dead as you'd like to see him. And isn't he ugly in death?"

"As ugly as his life ever was. I'd like to take my own out on him for once, if you don't mind," pleaded the rabbit.

"Oh, for sure. Please yourself. I myself have had the pleasure of punching him in the teeth a dozen times since I laid him flat on his back."

"He met his match this time, surely."

And with that, the rabbit drew near to hit Kue in the teeth. Kue leapt up, and in the twinkling of an eye, the rabbit lay at the bottom of the canoe, dead. Kuru laughed heartily and paddled ever faster. Kue lay down again and pretended to be dead.

The same fate that had befallen the antelope and the rabbit also befell a young hippo and a sea lion. At that point, Kuru suggested to Kue that they return home.

"Just one more animal," replied Kue. "Let's have enough for today and the next few weeks. Who knows how much longer the famine's going to last? And we may not be so lucky the next expedition around. As a matter of fact, I could do with some monkey meat."

"How d'you know we'll find a monkey?"

"Paddle on. We may be luckier than you think."

Kuru obeyed his friend. It did not take long before they saw a monkey sitting on a high branch. Kuru wept loudly, more loudly than he had done before. The monkey had never heard Kuru weep so loudly and he became a little suspicious.

"What's the matter?" asked the monkey of Kuru.

"It's Kue, the strong one."

"What happened to him?"

"He's dead. He died this morning of hunger, in his sleep. I'm taking him to his mother's so they can give him a decent burial."

"That's kind of you. Why should you do him such honor in death? He was always a most dishonorable fellow, as you well know."

"We have to honor the dead," Kuru answered through his tears.

"I see," said the monkey skeptically.

"Why don't you come down and pay him your final respects? Embrace him or slap him, whichever you wish to do. Either would please me very much."

"Right. I'll please myself for once. I'll come down right away."

"Quickly, quickly. I'm working against the tide. And Kue has to get to his mother before he begins to rot."

"I'll be with you in a minute," replied the monkey, jumping into another tree.

Kue looked more dead than ever, showing his teeth in a horrible grin of death, even as he braced himself to deal the monkey a fatal blow. He had been angered by the monkey describing him as a dishonorable fellow.

The monkey soon returned, a large object in his hand. He jumped to a lower branch.

"Are you coming down?" asked Kuru through his moan.

"Right away," answered the monkey. "Let me but adjust my dress properly."

He aimed carefully at Kue. He wanted to get him right in his shining teeth. In his hand was a huge coconut.

Kuru was getting impatient, as was Kue.

"Hurry up!" Kuru commanded.

This time, the monkey did not answer him. He merely hurled the coconut right into Kue's upturned face and hit home.

Kue was taken completely by surprise. He fell out of the canoe into the river. Kuru could not contain himself as Kue struggled in the river.

"Wha! wha! wha! wha!" laughed Kuru. "Wha! wha! wha!"

"Whe! whe! whe! whe!" laughed the monkey from the treetop.

"Wha! wha! wha! wha!" laughed Kuru as Kue, wet and angry, clambered into the canoe. He had taken a few gulps of water before he regained his place in the canoe. His eyes were red with anger. He promised to punish the monkey for his impertinence, some day. But he was even more angry at Kuru who was still laughing uncontrollably.

"I'll kill you if you don't shut your mouth this moment!" growled Kue.

"Wha! wha! wha! wha!" laughed Kuru.

"What's so funny?" demanded Kue, drawing near Kuru, a menacing look in his eyes.

Kuru continued to laugh. Kue made to pounce on him, and the skies immediately came down close to the waters and all grew dark. Remembering his promise, Kue relented. The skies drew back to the heavens and the sun shone once again.

"Forgive me, friend," Kuru pleaded, stifling another laugh, "if I cry at what should make me laugh. To cry is to show my teeth and to laugh is just the same. And I chose to cry this time, my dear friend."

Kue was not convinced. He said to himself that he would have to eat up Kuru some day. Then he ordered Kuru to turn the canoe round so they could return home.

As Kuru paddled home, he could still hear the monkey's laugh as he jumped into the thick of the forest, savoring his victory over Kue the Leopard.

Kue and Kuru shared the fruit of their hunting expedition equally and staved off their hunger that season of famine.

Had Kue not kept his promise to Kuru, the skies and the earth would have met and darkness would have buried the world.

It is proper that we keep our promise to our friends, no matter what. In this way, the world will be a better place.

Bibliography

Adotey Addo, Peter Eric. *Ghana Folk Tales: Ananse Stories from Africa.* New York: Exposition Press, 1968.
Aesop's Fables. Trans. V. S. Vernon Jones. Intro. G. K. Chesterton. Illust. Arthur Rackham. New York: Garden City Publishing, 1939.
Alfonso. Pedro. *The Scholar's Guide.* Trans. Joseph Ramon Jones and John Esten Keller. Toronto: Pontifical Institute of Medieval Studies, 1969.
Animal Fables of India: Narayana's Hitopadesha or Friendly Counsel. Trans. Francis G. Hutchins. West Franklin, New Hampshire: Amarta Press, 1985.
Awouma, Joseph Marie. *Contes et fables du Cameroun: Initiation à la littérature orale.* Yaoundé: Éditions Clé, 1976.
Babrius and Phaedrus. *Greek and Latin Fables in the Aesopic Tradition.* Ed. and trans. into English Ben Edwin Perry. Cambridge, Harvard University Press, 1965.
Bleek, W. H. I. *Reynard the Fox in South Africa: Hottentot Fables and Tales.* London: Trübner, 1864.
Calvino, Italo. *Italian Folktales.* Trans. George Martin. New York: Pantheon, 1956.
The Case of the Animals versus Man Before the King of the Jinn. Trans. from Arabic with intro. and commentary Lenn Evan Goodman. Boston: Twayne, 1978.
Chinese Fables. Ed. Ma Da. Beijing: Foreign Language Press. 1991.
Colette. *Creatures Great and Small; Creature Conversations; Other Creatures; Creature Comfort.* Trans. Enid McLeod. London: Secker and Warburg, 1951.
Fables of a Jewish Aesop Translated From the Fox Fables of Berechiah ha-Nakdan. Trans. Moses Hadas. New York: Columbia University Press, 1967.
Harris, Joel Chandler. *Told by Uncle Remus: New Stories of the Old Plantation.* Illust. A. B. Frost, J. M. Condé, and Frank Verbeck. New York: McClure, Phillips, 1905.
The Hungry Tigress: Buddhist Legends and Jataka Tales, versions of Rafe Martin. Berkeley, Calif.: Parallax Press, 1990.
Kai, Nubia. *The Sweetest Berry on the Bush: Tales & Fables.* Chicago: Third World Press, 1993.
Kalila and Dimna: Selected Fables of Bidpai. Retold by Ramsay Wood with an introduction by Doris Lessing. London: Granada, 1980.
Krilof and His Fables. Trans. W. R. S. Ralston. London: Strahan and Co. Publishers, 1869.
The Fables of La Fontaine. Trans. Into English Walter Thornbury. London: Cassell, Peter, and Galpin, 1871.
La Fontaine, Jean de. *Fables choisies mises en vers.* Paris, 1668.
La Fontaine, Jean de. *Fables choisies mises en vers.* Ed. Ferdinand Gohin. Paris:

Société Les Belles Lettres, 1934.
The Fables of Leonardo da Vinci. Trans. Bruno Nardini. New York: Harper Collins, 1973.
Lessing, Gotthold Ephraim. *Fables and Epigrams: With Essays on Fable and Epigram.* London: J. H. L. Hunt, 1825.
Lessing, Gotthold Ephraim. *Fabeln und Fabelabhandlungen, Werke und Briefe.* Ed. W. Barner et al. Frankfurt: Deutsher Klassiker Verlag, 1997.
Lopez, Barry. *Giving Birth to Thunder, Sleeping With His Daughter: Coyote Builds North America.* New York: Avon Books, 1990.
Mandeville, Bernard. *Fable of the Bees: Private Vices, Publick Benefits.* Oxford: F. B. Kaye, 1924.
Marie de France. *Fables.* Toronto: University of Toronto Press, 1987.
Montejo, Victor. *The Bird Who Cleans the World and Other Mayan Fables.* Willimantic, Conn.: Curbstone Press, 1991.
Muschio, Carla. *Da dove vengono i bambini? Where do children come from?* Viterbo: Millelire Stampa Alternativa, 1999.
The Panchatantra. Trans. Arthur W. Ryder. Chicago: University of Chicago Press, 1925.
Perrault, Charles. *Contes des fées.* English. *Histories or Tales of Past Times Told by Mother Goose.* Trans. G. M., Gent. London: Nonesuch, 1925.
Ruiz, Juan. *The Book of Good Love.* Trans. Saralyn R. Daly. University Park, Penn.: Pennsylvania State University Press, 1978.
Saro-Wiwa, Ken. *The Singing Anthill: Ogoni Folk Tales.* London, Lagos, Port Harcourt: Saros International Publishers, 1991.
Saroyan, William. *Saroyan's Fables.* New York: Harcourt Brace, 1941.
Sylvain, Georges. *Cric? Crac!: fables créoles.* Haiti: Éditions Fardin, 1901.
Thurber, James. *Fables for Our Time.* New York: Harper & Row, 1940.
Thurber, James. *Further Fables for Our Time.* New York: Simon and Schuster, 1956.
Tolstoy, Leo. *Fables and Fairy Tales.* Trans. Ann Dunnigan and illust. Sheila Greenwald and foreword by Raymond Rosenthal. New York: New American Library, 1962.

The Editors

Brenda Deen Schildgen is a Professor of Comparative Literature at the University of California, Davis. She has published widely on the European Middle Ages, specializing in medieval southern Europe, hermeneutics and interpretive theory, reception theory, and narrative theory. Her books include *Crisis and Continuity: Time in the Gospel of Mark*; *Power and Prejudice; The Reception of the Gospel of Mark*, *Boccaccio's Decameron and Chaucer's Canterbury Tales*, a co-edited volume; *Pagans, Tartars, Jews, and Moslems in Chaucer's Canterbury Tales*, and *Dante and the Orient*.

Georges Van Den Abbeele is a scholar of early modern French literature and contemporary continental philosophy. He taught at Santa Cruz, Berkeley, Harvard and Miami Universities before coming to the University of California, Davis in 1990, where he chaired the Department of French and Italian from 1997 to 2001 and currently directs the Davis Humanities Institute and Humanities Programs.

He is the author of *Travel as Metaphor: From Montaigne to Rousseau* and of *Utopias of Difference: For a Genealogy of the French Intellectual* (forthcoming from Stanford University Press). He is also the translator of Jean-Francois Lyotard's *The Differend: Phrases in Dispute*, *Postmodern Fables*, and *Enthusiasm: The Kantian Critique of History*. He is the co-editor with Tyler Stovall of *French Civilization and its Discontents: Nationalism, Colonialism, Race*. He has also guest-edited a number of special issues: on travel literature (*L'Esprit Créateur*, 1985; *Sites*, 2001), on Lyotard (*Diacritics*, 1984), and on censorship (*Diacritics*, 1997).